DANNY'S DOUBLE

A DANNY AND PARK NOVEL

AUTHOR'S NOTE

This novel is a work of fiction. However, it is based on actual crimes that occurred in the City of Richmond during the years the author was a police officer there. The names of all involved have been changed to protect their identities. The methods of fugitive apprehension have also been changed to make sure no advantage is given to criminals on the run.

In one of the action scenes, an officer fires a gun through the windshield of his car. This is not fiction and has happened in numerous situations, most recently in an incident that was captured on BWC (Body Worn Camera) in Las Vegas. Check it out online; it's amazing.

Finally, while Richmond, Virginia is of course a real city, some of its geography has been changed to meet the storytelling needs of the author.

I hope you enjoy the book.

JPB

Acknowledgements

I'd like to thank my family and friends who've read through my initial version of this book and pointed out misspellings, grammar mistakes, and some continuity issues. Like sage advice given to lawyers about having a fool for a client if you represent yourself, an author most definitely should NOT proofread his own work! Thanks, MF, JG, BG, and KNM.

Glossary of words/abbreviations used in the novel

10-1: Weak radio transmission

10-2: Good radio transmission

10-4: Everything is ok

10-5: Relay to. When one officer is trying to talk to another officer over a police channel, an officer will ask the dispatcher to '10-5' to the officer they are trying to speak to. For example, if Unit #113 wants to talk to Unit #114, the transmission would be, "113, 10-5 to 114." The dispatcher would then repeat what 113 just said and wait for 114 to answer.

10-6: Busy. If an officer is in the middle of something and can't meet up nor talk, that officer is '10-6.'

10-7: To be out of service. If a police unit is on a call or otherwise tied up, they're 10-7. In police slang, it can also mean dead; i.e. 'The victim is 10-7.'

10-8: Back in service, done with the call

10-9: Repeat. As in, repeat what you just said. For example, "114 to 113, 10-9. I couldn't hear you."

10-10: Negative/no

10-11: The code an officer uses to let the dispatcher know that they are 'marking on duty', or available for calls

10-14: Information. When one officer wants to pass on information to other officers. "113 to radio? Copy some 10-14 on the robbery suspects."

10-17: En route. "113, I'm 10-17 to that call."

10-20: Location

10-21: Phone call. "113, 10-5 to 114? Can you give me a 10-21?"

10-22: Disregard. "113 to 114? 10-22 that 10-21. I found out what I needed."

10-23: Arrived on scene. "113, I'm 10-23 at the robbery call."

10-25: Meet. "113 to 114? Can you 10-25 me at the robbery call?"

10-29: Checking to see if a person has active arrest warrants. "113 to radio? I need a 10-29 on a person."

10-31: Requesting a pick-up; usually picking up a prisoner but used sometimes casually used to pick up an officer. "113 to 114? Can you provide a 10-31 back from the garage? I need to drop off my car for service and need a ride back to the precinct."

10-33: Mayday or help me immediately. This code is rarely used in favor of 'Mayday' or 'I need more units now.'

10-96: Unofficial code for someone who is mentally unstable

DEC: Department of Emergency Communications. Police and fire dispatch, as well as the 911 call center.

BOLO: Be on the lookout

POV: Personally owned vehicle; an officer's personal car

GSW: Gunshot wound

EOT: End of tour; the end of an officer's workday

FTO: Field Training Officer; a seasoned officer who trains rookies

NUA: No Units Available; all police, fire or medic units are tied up on other calls

MDT: Mobile Data Terminal; mounted laptop computers in police cars

ASP baton: A collapsible, metal baton that replaced the wooden ones that RPD officers used to carry

OC: Oleoresin Capsicum; a much stronger form of the mace that officers used to carry. OC incapacitates by inflaming a person's eyes, nose and lungs.

PR: Personal Relief; bathroom break

BWC: Body Worn Camera

CHAPTER 1

"Damn, how about a courtesy flush?" Park asked as he walked into the 1st Precinct locker room at 0550hrs on his first day back to work after the three-day weekend. There was silence, then a throat clearing, and finally a flush. "Hit it again. Jesus Christ, it smells like decomp in here."

"Dammit!!" came the reply, as splashing came from the second stall away from the lockers, followed by the stall door banging open and Officer Scott Shook emerging from the stall in white boxer shorts and a black compression shirt. He waddled out bowlegged, trying to avoid stepping in the foul waterfall that seeped from the toilet. "Fuck, Shook!" Park bellowed. "That was the only stall that still worked!"

"It's not my fault!" Shook shouted back. "You made me flush twice. You know these old ass toilets can't take it." Shook was right. The precinct was practically falling apart. This was especially true in the locker room. The carpet hadn't been replaced in years; the lockers were all banged up and smelled like dirty laundry (on a good day). One corner of the floor to ceiling mirror on the wall opposite the lockers had cracked completely off, showing bare drywall underneath.

And then there were the toilets. Ah, the toilets. Of the three stalls, only two had ever worked in Park's twenty-two years as a patrol officer at 1st Precinct, his one and only assignment with the Richmond Police Department (his choice, by the way). When the second of the three had given up the ghost, the male officers made do with the one lone survivor. Alas, now this brave warrior had finally fallen. RIP brave toilet, and godspeed.

"Please tell me that the commode choked down whatever you put in there before it died," hoped Park.

"I think it did," answered Shook, looking around on the floor just to make sure. He'd hung his uniform up in his locker before going in the stall, fortuitously for him, as he wouldn't hit roll call with wet trouser legs. "Let the sarge know I may be a few minutes late to roll call," Shook stated, then wrapped a towel around his waist and headed to another toilet at the end of the hallway.

"Will do," Park muttered, getting out of there before his boots got wet. Just another morning at glorious 1st Precinct in Richmond's east end.

Anthony Osbourne had been planning his trip back to Richmond for months now. After Duane had gotten killed by that cop during the bank robbery, Anthony had had to make it back to Brooklyn on a shoestring budget. The original plan had been to go back in style with the money

from the bank robbery lining their pockets. But he never even got a single dollar bill from it. Once he got back to Brooklyn, the people that he and Duane borrowed money from to finance their bank robbery were not pleased to see Anthony back in Brooklyn empty handed. They didn't even seem to care that poor Duane got killed. Anthony wasn't too good at planning, but he wanted two things from Richmond: money and revenge.

CHAPTER 2

Det. Danny Jacobs' alarm went off at 0500hrs. Danny didn't have to leave his house until around 0700hrs to make it in for his Major Crimes day shift, but he liked to get up early to do some light weight training and some yoga. When he was younger and in a patrol car, he leaned to more heavy lifting and less, if any, stretching. Now at 43yrs old, his priorities had shifted. His joints were becoming stiff and painful, and his hips were starting to ache. He'd discovered that if he lifted lighter and stretched more, it was easier to move around and his knees and back weren't in constant pain. Getting older was less of a bitch when you could move around with less pain.

Two of his three cats, his only recent sleeping companions, hopped out of bed when he rolled out from under the sheets. His third cat had gone rogue and hadn't been seen for a week. He wasn't completely off the grid, though, since Danny had left food out on the deck. Once the wayward cat finished his meals, he'd leave a turd or two as a greeting. He had the entire yard to use as his toilet and he chose to use the deck. Each and every time, the fucker.

Workout, shower, shave for him, then breakfast for him and the cats. Morning tasks completed, he geared up and headed out to his car. He'd finally gotten his unmarked back. It had been months, but they'd been reunited. It was nice to turn the key and have the engine start right up and stay running. He'd gotten the car back just as the Bryan Park murder pleas were starting to come in. Christine Peck, the lead prosecutor, had prophesied correctly and the accomplices in the case got around forty years a piece while the shooter got life, plus fifteen. And Danny didn't even have to testify. He'd stayed in touch with the victim's family and they were satisfied with the pleas. Diane, the surviving witness, had moved back to Indiana and was considering a career in federal law enforcement. Overall, the best outcome of an awful incident.

Since Danny hadn't had any murders since the Bryan Park case, he was helping Det. Eric New out with identifying the remaining shooter from the Fidelity Bank robbery/murder a few months ago. New had been making some progress on associates of the guy killed by Officer Abad. Danny had been assisting with research and phone calls. So overall it had been a tranquil three months in the City of Richmond. Which is the last thought Danny had at a red light before a guy on a scooter rear-ended him and flew through his back window.

CHAPTER 3

"113 log and a unit to back, unit 113 and unit to back, respond to 1104 N. 30th St. and see the complainant in reference to a missing person. Complainant is at the address and sees carpet removed and possibly blood on the floor. 113 and a unit to back, respond code 2," transmitted the dispatcher on RPD police channel 1.

"113 copies from the precinct," Park responded. He looked in his rearview mirror and saw Shook right behind him, loading up his car. Shook pointed to his chest, then to Park and then to his radio mic. Park nodded and said, "116's with me and he'll take my back."

"10-4, 113 and 116. Your complainant's name is Clifford Minor. He says the person missing is Bernadette Oliver."

"10-4, radio. Enroute," Park replied. He got on the car's PA system and said, "I'll meet you over there, Shook." Shook gave him a thumbs up and Park started rolling out of the lot. Sergeant Rooney banged out of the side door and yelled, "Yo, Park! Hold up!" Park rolled to a stop and Rooney jogged up to the car. "Hey, Park. Give me a call when you find out what's going on over there. Sounds ominous with blood on the floor and carpet torn up."

"Will do, sarge," Park replied. "Hey, do you know if there are any tracking dogs on the line-up today? May come in handy."

"I'll make some calls and see. Here comes Shook. Take it easy and fill me in as soon as you can." Park nodded and he and Shook took a right out of the precinct lot and drove the five blocks to the house, not feeling any positive vibes about Bernadette Oliver's fate.

* * *

"113 and 116 are 10-23," Park transmitted as they arrived at the house. A middle-aged man came over to Park's car as he was getting out. "Officers, I'm glad you're here. Man, I'm worried to death about Bernie," the man stated, a thick New Jersey accent punctuating his words.

"Bernie is Bernadette?" Park asked.

"Yeah," the man replied.

"And who are you?" Park asked. Shook had gotten out of his car and was standing slightly behind and to the side of Park; taking up a tactical position. This was just a missing person case right now, but things went sideways quickly, and cops always had to be ready for an ambush.

"Oh, sorry. I'm Clifford Minor. You can call me Cliff. I've known Bernie for years. We grew up together in Plainfield, New Jersey. She still lives up there. I moved down here about ten years ago."

"Whose house is this, if she lives in New Jersey?" Park asked.

"I don't know who actually owns it, but the guy who rents it is Andrew Billups," Minor replied.

"And who is Billups to Bernie?" Park asked. This was starting to get convoluted and he could feel a headache coming on.

"Well, Andy is friends with Bernie's boyfriend, Edward Troy."

"Let me see if I got this straight," Park began. "Billups rents this place here in Richmond. Billups is friends with Edward Troy, who is Bernadette's boyfriend. Bernadette, who you call Bernie, is the person who's missing. Right?"

"Right!" said Minor. "Oh, and Edward might be missing, too."

"Jesus Christ," Shook muttered.

"When you called 911, you just mentioned Bernadette being missing. Now Edward is missing too?" Park asked. "I don't really know Eddie like that," said Minor. "I just know him through Bernie. When I called up to Plainfield to talk to Bernie's mom about if she'd seen Bernie, her mom said that she was supposed to be coming to Richmond with Eddie."

Still confused, Park waited for him to continue.

"So, once she told me *that*, she said that she'd call Eddie's people and see if they'd heard from him. If they had, then she could ask him where her daughter was. She called me back and said his people hadn't heard from him in days."

15

"And they didn't make a missing person report on him?" Park asked. "Well......see.....Eddie's a drug dealer and makes runs up and down the east coast. It's not unusual for him to be off the grid for a day or so. But when his people hadn't heard from him, then found out Bernie's mom hadn't heard from her either? They got a bad feeling," Minor said.

"And," Park finished for him, "His people thought that the police wouldn't take a missing drug dealer seriously, so they decided to roll him in with the missing woman, Bernie. That sound about right? So, Bernie and Edward are missing. Billups had nothing to do with anything; he just rents the house, right?"

"I guess so," Minor said, meaning, Park knew, that was exactly what happened. "Let's go look in the house," Park said.

CHAPTER 4

Danny was leaning on the hood of his car, left hand holding a cold rag against the back of his neck while his right hand rested casually on his gun. The guy who'd sailed through his back window was sitting on the bumper of the ambulance, one of the medics shining a penlight in his eyes. The guy's scooter was a crumpled mess that was partially embedded in Danny's rear bumper; the fluid leaking from it had slowed to a few drips. The fire department had hosed down the mess and was folding up their hoses getting ready to head back to their station.

"Damn, Danny," Detective Sergeant Ryan Dean said. "When it comes to cars, this one in particular, if you didn't have bad luck you wouldn't have any luck at all."

"No shit, Ryan," Danny responded. "I can't believe that guy survived. All he's got is some cuts from the glass, but the medics don't even think he broke any bones."

"I was over there listening to him as he was telling the Traffic guys what happened," Dean responded. "He saw you at the light, but when he tried to brake? Nothing. He Fred Flintstoned it but all that did was wear down his shoes." Danny looked over at the guy and lifted his chin in a greeting. The guy looked back and gave Danny the finger. "What the hell?" Danny asked. "He's blaming me because *he* crashed into *me*?"

"Yeah," Dean said. "According to him, if you hadn't stopped short, he could have stopped in time. So, he's probably going to sue the city for a new scooter, medical costs, and mental distress."

"Yeah, right," Danny said and started counting out points on his right hand. "One, I was stopped at a red light. Two, that scooter was probably made in 1990 and can't be worth more than twenty dollars. Three, it looks like his medical costs will be for Bactine and bandages. And four, he was probably already 'mentally distressed....'"; here he paused and raised his voice, so the guy could hear him, "BECAUSE HE'S RIDING ON A PIECE OF SHIT SCOOTER!!"

"Fuck YOU!!" yelled the guy. Then to the medics, "Can you guys take me to St. Mary's instead of the University hospital? St. Mary's got better food." The lead medic rolled her eyes and helped him into the back of the ambulance.

"That make you feel better, Danny?" Dean asked. "You'll probably get a complaint from one of these civilians standing around out here."

"Whatever," Danny said, removing the rag from the back of his head. When the guy came through the window, some safety glass must have come with him and scratched Danny's head. Before Dean could say anything else, Danny's phone rang. He looked at the phone's screen; Park. "Hey,

Park. What's up? Guess what happened to my car." Danny listened for a second, then patted himself down for a pad and a pen. "Uh-huh.... uh-huh.... boyfriend........ and girlfriend?... yeah.... uh-huh....... what's the address? Ok. Let me find a car and I'll be there in a few. What's that? No, I'll give Forensics a call and have them meet us over there." Danny hung up and turned to Dean. "I need a car."

Anthony couldn't sleep at night; he kept having flashbacks of the shootout at the bank. He'd been hustling people for years, running cons, ripping people off. He'd done some shoplifting and even some break-ins when the people who lived in the houses weren't home. But nothing ever violent. Until the bank in Richmond. Something got into him when he had that rifle in his hand; it made him feel powerful and completely in control. When that guy tried to make a run for the rear entrance and Anthony had shot him in the head, Anthony had gotten a crazy rush. Shooting that guy had just felt right. Anthony wasn't having a hard time sleeping because he felt bad about the shooting and gun play; he couldn't sleep because he missed it and wanted more.

CHAPTER 5

When Park and Shook looked in the window of the house and saw the carpet ripped up and the brown stains on the floor, Park stepped back from the window and gave Rooney a call. He didn't want to put it over the radio, because the media still had access to the police channels, and he didn't want them showing up until notifications were made up the chain. After hanging up with Rooney, he called Danny to let him know what was going on. He wasn't sure if Danny would get the case, but he'd know who in Major Crimes to notify.

"Did you go in the house?" Park asked Minor.

"No, I just looked in the window. I don't have a key," Minor replied.

"Ok, go stand over there by my car. We're going to have a look inside," Park directed. Minor walked over to the police car, dialing his cell phone as he went. "C'mon, Shook. Let's go clear the place real quick before the show starts."

"Shouldn't we wait for the detectives and Forensics?" Shook asked. He wasn't hesitating out of fear; he just didn't want to contaminate a potential crime scene. "We would if

Minor had already gone and looked around inside," Park said. "But since he hasn't, we need to make sure no one's hiding in there. How'd you like to explain one of our Forensic people getting shot by a suspect still hiding in the house?" Shook acknowledged the point with a nod, then Park got up on the air:

"113 to radio. Give us the air. We need to do a quick search of the house."

"10-4, 113. Units hold the air for 113 and 116. Need K-9, 113?"

"Negative, radio. 10-10. Just making sure it's secure."

"Let's go, Shook." They went up to the front door and both put on the rubber gloves they keep in pouches on their belts. They were hot as hell, but you could still maintain your grip with them on, as well as get a good feel on the trigger. Plus, since they were trying to keep scene contamination to a minimum, anything they had to touch inside wouldn't get their prints nor DNA on it. Park turned the doorknob and found it unlocked. Before going in, he told Shook to wait and went back to his car. He brought back two pairs of Tyvek booties that they both slid over their boots, so they wouldn't track anything in. They pulled their guns, held them in low-ready, and went into the house.

* * *

Danny had caught a ride to the office from Dean so he could pick up the "junker," a spare car that Major Crimes was allowed to use. He'd been stuck with it for the past eight months, and now it looked like he'd be stuck with it for a few months longer. He grabbed the keys off the board and walked up to the top of the parking deck to get it and park it in the shade. He left it idling so the weak AC could *hopefully* cool down the interior before he drove to meet Park. He had an idea and called Park, who answered on the third ring.

"Hey, Danny. I was just getting ready to call you. Shook and I just got done clearing the house. No bad guys inside, but you can smell the old blood in there. There may be some in the hall bathroom, too. The only thing we touched was the doorknob, but we had gloves on. Booties, too. We left gloves and booties in a bag by the front door."

"Thanks, Park. Do me a favor? While I'm at the office, I'm going to go on and type up a search warrant for the house, based on what that guy told you and what you saw. Forensics is on the way to you, along with my partner, Taylor. There may be a few other detectives and my sergeant as well."

Park rolled his eyes as he listened. As he predicted, it was going to turn into a circus.

"Do me a favor and describe the house to me; one story or two, brick or siding, where the house numbers are located. Like that," Danny said. Park called Shook over and put Danny on speakerphone. "Say all that shit again, Danny. I'm going to let Shook get involved here. Good training for him."

"Dammit, Park," Danny started to say, but then repeated what he'd just said to Shook. Danny hung up and Park put the phone back in his pocket. "Why did he need such specific information for the search warrant?" Shook asked. "Couldn't he just put the address in the affidavit?"

"Because," explained Park, "That's been done in the past and typos have been made that listed a completely different house. Say your target is 4-5-2-9, but the officer or detective is tired and accidentally types 4-9-2-5. That's four blocks away and the wrong house. So, you kick in that door and give a granny a heart attack. Boom. Lawsuit. This way, you load up all of the descriptors in the affidavit and make sure you get the right house."

"Makes sense," Shook said. As they'd been talking, unmarked units began pulling up, along with the forensic van and the brass. "You go start typing up the report," Park said. "I'm going to try and get us out of here, so we can take care of these pending calls. Plus, I want to swing by the Property Room and check on Abad. I'm sure he's going crazy down there." Shook got into the car and started typing, while Park walked over to Rooney to get cut loose and get far, far away from the shit show.

CHAPTER 6

After speaking with Park, Danny had made some follow up calls to the cops in New Jersey and found out that Edward Troy had a wife in Jersey who had reported him missing. She had heard that Bernadette had been shot and killed in Richmond but could not (or would not) say where she got that information. She had already made a missing person report for her husband in New Jersey. A patrol officer in Jersey had also found out from Bernadette's employer that she had a boyfriend named "Edward" who was a drug dealer. In addition, the officer had found that Bernadette had rented a car just before leaving Jersey, presumably to drive down to Richmond. Clearly, there was a lot of sketchy stuff going on with these two. Danny included all of this in the probable cause section of the search warrant and looked over what he'd typed:

4. The material facts constituting probable cause that the search should be made are:

The Richmond Police Department was called to 1104 N. 30th St. on a suspicious situation. Once on scene, Officer Chester Park spoke with the complaint Simon Minor of Richmond, Virginia. Minor was trying to locate a friend by the name of Bernadette Oliver, female, DOB: 6-17-1971. According to Minor, he had last spoken to Oliver in Plainfield, New Jersey. Minor stated Oliver had rented a car: Nissan Altima, 4dr, silver in color, N.J. tag to drive to Virginia. Oliver told him she was coming to 1104 N. 30th St.

Minor also stated she left New Jersey with Edward Troy.

Minor told Officer Park that he had been by the house and no one was home, but he peeked through the window and saw what looked like a piece of the carpet had been cut out from the floor. Minor felt something had happened to his friend Oliver.

Sergeant Rooney contacted the leaseholder, an Andrew Billups, who stated he had not been to the house in over a month and was out of town. Billups told Sergeant Rooney that he had a roommate named Edward Troy.

Your affiant was contacted by Officer J. Furdo of the Plainfield Police Department in New Jersey. Officer Furdo advised he had responded to 276 Watchtog Avenue, Plainfield, New Jersey, on a "Welfare Check" for a Bernadette Oliver. The complaints were leaseholders, a Yvonne Taylor and Dewayne Sobetrs. They stated they were unable to get in touch with Bernadette Oliver for the past four or five days. Officer Furdo entered the apartment and did not locate Oliver. Officer Furdo stated in his police report the apartment was neat and there were no signs of a physical altercation.

Officer Furdo also spoke with an unidentified, close friend of Oliver's, who stated he was unable to get in touch with Oliver for the past four of five days.

Officer Furdo spoke with Officer Hendrickson, Plainfield PD, who knew Oliver's employer. The victim's employer told Officer Hendrickson that Oliver had gone to Richmond, Virginia, so she could renew her driver's license. Officer Hendrickson spoke with an unidentified co-worker, who stated the victim had maintained a relationship with a male named "Edward," who is a known drug dealer.

Officer Furdo states in his report, after checking booking records, they show Oliver having a Tattoo on her back with the name "Edward."

Your affiant received a fax copy of a "Missing Person" report from Plainfield Police Department, New Jersey, from a Sergeant Leslie Burgess. The report stated that a Mrs. Phillips said her husband, Edward Troy, left for Richmond, Virginia. Mrs. Phillips states that it was very uncommon for Troy not to contact her. Mrs. Phillips also stated that she heard that "Oliver's" body had been found in Richmond, Virginia, and she was shot and killed, but had not heard that of Troy.

Mr. Troy has been entered into NCIC as a missing person by Plainfield Police Department.

Officer Chester Park went to 1104 N. 30th St. and found the front door closed but unlocked. Officer Park and Officer Shook cleared the apartment for any danger and found blood and missing carpet.

Based on your affiant's training and experience, your affiant believes that person(s) trying to hide evidence of a crime could and have used carpets to hide a body for transportation, to a more secluded area without being detected by police.

Danny read it twice, printed it off and took it over to the Magistrate's Office. He raised his hand, swore that everything in the affidavit was true to the best of his knowledge and laid it out for her. Then, search warrant in hand, he called Taylor, his partner, and let him know he was on the way over with the warrant. Before he went over, he put out a BOLO (Be On the Lookout) for the rental car Bernadette was last seen driving. Five minutes later, he was standing just outside the house with Taylor and Dean. "Any word on what they've found so far?" Danny asked.

"Blood throughout the apartment and on the walls," Taylor said. "There's a black leather chair in the living room with blood on the arms. And there's a bathmat draped over the tub that's soaked in blood."

"Things aren't looking good for our missing New Jersey couple," Dean surmised. "No, they sure aren't," agreed Danny, as he looked at Simon sitting on the curb with his head buried in his hands.

Three hours later, the Forensics Team was done at the house and had found nothing else of significance with the exception of some bleach bottles under the sink. The techs could smell bleach in the living room and bathroom, which was consistent with someone cleaning up a crime scene. Danny had called up to the rental car company in New Jersey to see if the car had GPS on it; many companies did this in case the cars were not returned. Just not *that* rental company. A canvass had been done of the neighborhood, but no one saw nor heard anything suspicious. Taylor reached out to the city's Public Works to see when trash in the neighborhood was collected. It wouldn't be the first time a murderer put a body in a city 'super can' and hoped for a burial at a landfill. But trash pick-up wasn't scheduled until the day after tomorrow. Danny, Taylor, and a few patrol officers had searched the alleys, peeking into trashcans but had come up empty. Danny needed something to break.

CHAPTER 7

"116, break! We need some more units to our '20!" Shook transmitted. He and Park had responded to Phaup St. in Fairfield Court, a housing community in east Richmond. When they arrived, they had met the complainant at the door. Her shirt was torn, and her eye was swollen to a slit.

"Who did this to you? How'd it happen?" Park had asked.

"It was Tommy," she'd said. "That fucker came over here without the baby formula. I told him I needed some, like yesterday. My baby's hungry. He said he'd bring some over today. Instead he came over smelling like weed with no money in his pockets. No formula, either." She started pulling her shirt away from her body, assessing the damage. "Fuck! I just got this from the Maxx." In the background, a baby started crying, then another kid's voice hollering for his or her mom. "Shut the fuck up!! I'm talking!!" she screamed back.

"You talk to your kid like that?" Shook had asked. "What?" she'd responded. Shook just shook his head and turned his back to her. "Is that his kid in there?" Park had asked. "Yeah, the little one is his. I shit out the other one from another guy."

"Jesus Christ," Shook muttered and walked off the porch. Park ignored him and told her, "We're going to have to charge him for hitting you. You two have a kid in common. That makes it an automatic arrest on a domestic violence charge."

"Whatever man. I just need some formula and now a new shirt. Take that fucker to jail."

"You need an ambulance to look you over? Your eye's all swollen up," Park had asked. "Nah," she'd stated. "I'll be ok. I'm taking the baby to the university hospital later today, so I can go by the ER while I'm down there. Where do I go to take out the warrant?"

"We'll take care of it for you. I'll……," Park began, but she interrupted him and yelled, "There he goes right there! The guy in the yellow shirt!"

Shook had heard this and started walking to the guy. "Hey! You! Come here," Shook had stated. The guy looked at him, paused for a second, then took off running. Shook ran after him, gaining fast as they both went through the 'cut' (the space between two buildings). Park hopped off the porch and ran after both of them. When Park got through the cut, he saw that Shook had tackled the guy in front of another set of apartments. The guy wasn't giving up, so Shook was having a hard time getting him handcuffed. Park ran up beside him and added his weight to the pile, but the guy had stiff-armed like a modified push-up and wasn't going to the ground. A crowd had started to form around them, and they were quickly becoming outnumbered. Which was when Shook called for additional units.

Two tones on the radio, then: "All units, 116 has requested additional units to the 2000 block of Phaup St. Respond code 1."

Park had locked *his* arm through the guy's arm, and almost had it in control. Neither Park nor Shook were able to get their ASP out because the battle was in such close quarters and they needed some space to extend the baton. Their OC wouldn't work either; too close to the guy (police no longer use 'mace'; it's now OC – Oleo Capsicum or pepper spray). While Park was struggling with the guy's arms, he heard glass breaking near him. Then he felt something hit the back of his leg; not real painful, more of an annoyance. "Park! The crowd's throwing bottles at us!!" Shook yelled. Park lowered his head into the guy's back, hoping to get some protection from the bottles raining down. He could hear the sirens over the angry shouts of the crowd, but not the jangling of police equipment, the battle-rattle, that means the cavalry has arrived. Where the *fuck* was their backup?

* * *

"K-5, I'm 10-23 on Phaup St., but I don't see them," K9 Officer Sharon Wright transmitted; her partner, Thunder, barking in the background. If she'd driven into the subdivision from the Fairfield Ave. side, she would have driven right past the gathering crowd and figured out what was going on. Unfortunately for Park and Shook, she came in from the Cool Lane side, so she had no idea what was going on a block over.

"117, I'm 10-23 as well," Officer Percy Smith said, as he pulled in behind Sharon's SUV. Percy was 5''10" and nearly 260lbs; most of it muscle. He and Park had been in the academy together and he was chomping at the bit to find him.

"Radio calling? What's your 10-20? Units are on scene and trying to find you," the dispatcher quiered. She pulled up their cars on GPS and saw them parked on Phaup St. "Radio to K-5 or 117? Are their cars parked on Phaup St.?"

"10-4, radio," Sharon answered. "The cars are here, they're not."

Before the dispatcher could respond, a unit said, "112 to radio! I found them! They're over here on Selden Street. We need to clear out this crowd." While he was talking, you could hear the crowd yelling in the background. Sharon and Percy didn't bother with getting back on the radio and letting the dispatcher know they were going to Selden Street; the dispatcher knew they were going.

When they got there, they saw that Shook and Park had the guy on the ground and were in the process of getting him cuffed. Officer Warren Anderson, unit #112, had pushed himself through the crowd and was standing guard over Shook and Park, ASP out and ready to use it to hit someone or take a swing at a bottle if another came sailing through the air. Percy bulled his way through the crowd as well, knocking people down as he went using elbows and shoulders.

Sharon left Thunder in the car, making sure the door locked, and waded through the crowd as well. Thunder saw her go without him and barked and pawed at the door to get out into the action. Sharon couldn't have let him out just to sic him on anyone in the crowd, though. Some in the crowd were just watching, not actively trying to assault the officers. So, Thunder had to be an impatient observer. More police units arrived and were slowly bringing the situation under control. One of the latecomers had pulled out an OC fogger; this was a large container of OC that you either sprayed at people's feet, or over their heads in the air. The officer fired a quick burst in the air toward the center of the crowd and people smelled it, then started to disperse. Park and Shook had the guy cuffed and sitting on his ass on the ground. Park's shoulder mic had fallen off during the struggle, so he picked it up and let the dispatcher know that everyone was ok, including the bad guy, and to roll a paddy wagon to them. Sharon heard Park's transmission and saw him clip the mic back on his lapel. As she started walking back to the SUV, she heard Thunder barking, then saw a guy with a baseball bat getting ready to break the window to Thunder's compartment. "Hey, motherfucker!!" she yelled, running to stop him.

CHAPTER 8

Danny had just finished his lunch in the break room when he heard the officer-needs-assistance call on channel 1, meaning 1st Precinct. He turned his radio up and listened to it unfold. He heard Park get on the air and say that everyone was ok and to roll a wagon. Glad that his friend and the other officers were ok, he turned his radio off and checked out an email he'd gotten while he had been eating lunch:

FROM: burgesslplainfiieldpd.org

TO: Daniel.jacobs@richmondpd.gov

SUBJECT: Suspect info re: Oliver

Received information from Aubrey Mansfield, Bernadette's father, stating the following: he spoke with Edwards' father Irwin Troy who said he spoke with a male identified as Dennis Defreitis of Virginia who said he saw Edward at the 30th St. address but left in the morning. Dennis is said to also be in possession of the keys to the residence. Dennis is definitely a person of interest. Dennis told Edwards' father that both of them are dead. He provided details of how they were killed, stating Bernadette was shot in the chest while sleeping and Edward was shot in the head. Dennis made mention of accidentally burning money belonging to

> *Edward<u> that was placed in </u>an<u> oven in the </u>residence.<u> He also crashed </u>a<u> car belonging to </u>Edward<u> that is said to still be somewhere</u><u> in the </u>30th *St. neighborhood.<u> Also, </u>Dennis<u> is on parole out of Florida.</u>*

Danny checked the database and found that a Dennis Defreitis had been involved in a car accident about a month ago. He called the tow lot and found out that it had been towed to an address in south Richmond. Danny checked the database again and got a name and phone number for a woman who lived at that address. He dialed the number, introduced himself after a woman answered the phone, then asked if the car was still over at her house.

"It sure is," she said. "It belongs to some dude named Red." Danny glanced at the fact sheet he had up on his computer for Defreitis and under the AKA (also known as) icon it had RED listed as a nickname. "He asked me if he could leave it in the yard until he gets it fixed," she continued. "Now it's been here for weeks and it's got grass growing all around it. I just want it out of my yard."

"I think I can help you out," Danny said, then called up the number for the city's contract tow company.

* * *

After doing a little digging through DMV, Danny found that the abandoned car wasn't registered to Defreitis after all. He looked up the registered owner's name and gave him a call. As it turns out, the owner had lent 'Red' the car weeks ago and he'd never returned it. The owner hadn't made a stolen car report yet since he had known 'Red' for years and wanted to give him a chance to return it.

"Well," Danny said. "He's not going to return it to you because he wrecked it and left it to rot in a lady's yard over on south side."

"That's some fucking bullshit!" the guy yelled, making Danny pull the phone away from his ear. "I want that fucker charged with stealing my car!!" Since he'd said that he'd known 'Red' for years, Danny texted him a single photo of Defreitis and got immediate confirmation that he was the person who 'borrowed' the car.

Danny gave the owner a report number and called over to the prosecutor's office to let Christine Peck know what was going on. When she got on the line, he gave her all the background information, then said, "So I like this guy for killing Bernadette and Edward, then getting rid of their bodies. Probably some kind of drug rip, based on Edward's history. I don't have enough to charge him with the murders yet."

"Plus, we don't have the bodies," Peck added.

"Plus, that," Danny said. "But I do have enough to charge him with the auto theft and get Cindy on him."

Cindy was a Richmond detective who had been sworn in federally to work with the U.S. Marshals on fugitive captures. "I'm on board with that," Peck said. "Just keep me in the loop." Danny hung up with her, then called Cindy. He was on a roll now.

Anthony still had the rifle that he'd used in the bank robbery. Well, he had it, but not with him. He knew the gun laws were much stricter in New York than in Virginia, and the penalties were harsher. So, on the drive back from Richmond, he'd had to get off the highway a few times and take back roads. On one of the back roads in Maryland, he'd seen a vacant house and went in to look. It seemed to him like no one had been in it for years. He checked the floors and found some loose boards in one of the smaller bedroom closets. He popped the board up, used a stick to knock cobwebs out of the way, then stashed the rifle in there. He made sure that he wrapped it up in the reversible shirt he'd worn in the robbery. He wondered if it was still there. Only one way to find out: road trip.

CHAPTER 9

When Sharon was running up to the guy who was getting ready to smash Thunder's window, she wasn't thinking calmly and coolly like the professional cop she was. Instead, she was running hot, full of rage at the motherfucker who was getting ready to hurt her partner. The guy had missed the window on his first swing, hitting the quarter panel below it instead, putting a good-sized dent in the SUV. He was rearing back for the second swing when he sensed Sharon coming. He adjusted his grip and drove the handle of the bat straight into Sharon's stomach. Sharon did CrossFit, but the strike caught her off guard and she doubled over. The guy then launched his knee straight up, catching her in the chin, knocking her backwards onto the ground. She crab-walked back trying to get away from him long enough to get her bearings. The entire time, Thunder was barking like mad, tearing at the interior of the car to get to Sharon.

* * *

The scene was so hectic and so many people were around, the other cops didn't realize Sharon was in a knock-down, drag-out fight. They heard Thunder barking in the background, but knew that their K9s barked like crazy nearly all the time, so they figured that was Thunder being Thunder, so they kept dispersing the crowd unaware of what was unfolding.

The guy swung the bat at Sharon again, hitting her in the shoulder. She'd kicked out and caught him in the side of his knee, knocking him off balance mid-swing. He fell on her and gripped the bat in both hands, forcing all his weight onto the bat, getting closer to her neck. She kept her left hand on the bat and reached her right hand down to a small device on her belt that had a large button on it. She pushed the button, causing Thunder's door to spring open by remote control. Thunder came roaring out of the SUV and launched himself onto the guy's back, ripping and tearing at his arms, torso, and ass. When the guy started screaming like he was on fire, the other cops on scene looked over, did a double take at seeing Sharon on the ground and Thunder tearing into the guy like a chew toy, then hauled ass over to her. But by then, Thunder had it all under control.

CHAPTER 10

Danny was at the printer down the hall from his office when he heard his cell phone ringing; he'd left it on his desk to charge. He got back to it just as it stopped ringing, natch. He glanced at the screen and saw that it had been Cindy trying to reach him. He tugged the charging cord from the bottom of the phone and called her back. "Sorry, Cindy. Phone was charging, and I was down the hall. What's up?"

"Hey. I just got the wanted poster and US Marshal Form about this Defreitis guy. Is this a good phone number for him?" Cindy asked. Phone numbers were always a good starting place when looking for fugitives. Determining if the phone was active, what numbers it was calling, and which numbers were calling it, all helped paint a picture of where the target may be. If a detective didn't have a good phone number, Cindy wasn't happy.

"I think that's going to be the most recent number for him," Danny confirmed. "I checked the database we use that aggregates all the phone numbers with addresses and names and got a hit on the number I gave you. When he wrecked the stolen car, that's the number he gave the officer working the accident."

"And is this guy a Virginia dude or a New York guy?" Cindy asked.

"I think he's a New York guy mainly. The information I'm getting is he's part of a drug network that's going up and down the east coast. If he goes all the way down to Florida, he probably uses Virginia as a mid-way point. Like a rest stop. He's got a record in Maryland, too."

"Ok," Cindy said. "We'll get up on his phone and see what's going on with it. Hopefully he's in Richmond so we can nab him sooner than later. They found any bodies, yet?"

"Nope. But per my Plainfield sergeant, word's all over Brooklyn that they're dead. Bernadette shot in the chest, Edward in the head."

"That's pretty specific," Cindy replied.

"It is," Danny agreed. "Hopefully the car that she rented turns up somewhere. You remember that car from the Bryan Park murder? They burned it and fucked up any evidence that may have been in there."

"Right. Well, we'll let you know here soon how we're looking with this guy's phone. Gotta go." Click. Cindy wasn't a fan of lengthy conversations when she *wasn't* looking for a fugitive. When she was hunting, count on a two-minute convo, max. Danny wasn't offended. He had plenty to keep him busy and got back to it. Since Defreitis had ties and a possible address in New York, Danny called up to the NYPD and got put in touch with a Sgt. John Simons, a member of their Intelligence Unit. Simons ran Defreitis' name through

NYPD's system and got a few minor hits (traffic tickets plus a couple of trespassing cases) but no drug nexus. Simons said that he'd put them on their radar and agreed to be a POC (point of contact) for Danny when he needed to get some more information. He suggested that Danny check the LPR database. License plate readers were being used more and more frequently by law enforcement, insurance companies, and bail bondsmen. A car could be outfitted with the LPRs on both sides, front, and back. The cars would then cruise up and down streets while the LPRs recorded every license plate on the vehicles the LPR car passed. Afterward, all the data would be uploaded to a shared database. The site was quickly becoming invaluable in locating cars. Danny thanked him and hung up, then put a call in to one of the RPD's crime analysts about the LPRs.

Cindy had run the suspect number Danny had given her through her cell phone contacts and found out that the phone *was* active and *was* registered to Defreitis. Since Defreitis had an active felony warrant out and since she had gotten the phone confirmation, she got a search warrant to locate the physical location of the phone. Hopefully it would be with Defreitis and not left behind in his apartment while he was out moving around with a 'burner' phone (burners are cheap, prepaid phones that can be bought just about everywhere. They're practically impossible to trace. Though

Cindy was a miracle worker and had traced more than one burner in her career.) Within the hour, Cindy had the search warrant served and had tracked the phone. It was currently showing stationary at an address on Hull St. in Richmond's south side. Cindy put the address in an internet search engine and brought up the street view map. "Well now," she said, looking at the computer screen. "There you are, Mr. Defreitis. Sitting at Sugar Daddy's Sugar Shack. One of Richmond's nastiest strip joints." She picked up the phone and called Danny.

Anthony felt something sticky on the steering wheel. Blood he guessed. When he stabbed the driver in the back of the head with the kitchen knife, the guy flopped forward, blood spraying out like a faucet. Anthony had gotten one of those burner smart phones, then put the ride app on it. He got picked up near the waterfront in Red Hook, then waited until they came to an isolated area near the Gowanus and drove the knife right into the back of his head while they were at a red-light. It went in surprisingly easy, sounded kind of like squeezing a handful of Rice Krispies. But the blood.....holy shit! He'd cleaned it up the best he could with the guy's shirt and some wipes he'd found in the glove compartment. He got out of the back seat, dragged the guy out, and shoved him behind a dumpster. He pulled the guy's cell phone off of the dashboard and threw it on the ground next to his body. He went through the whole package of wipes and thought he'd done a pretty good job until he started driving and felt the stickiness on his hands.

No big deal, he'd just stop at some convenience store in Baltimore on the way to get his rifle, clean up a little more. And the body? He wasn't planning on coming back to Brooklyn anytime soon. And he was starting to get a taste for killing. He wanted to spread it around.

CHAPTER 11

"I fucked up, Park," Shook admitted. "I should have told dispatch that our location changed when I went to chase that guy." They were standing outside the ambulance where Sharon was getting looked over. Thunder was on the bench beside her, panting and smiling. He had one paw on Sharon's thigh while the medic was gently pressing on her stomach and ribs. Sharon had removed her shirt and vest and Shook stole a glance or two at her while he was apologizing to Park. Shook considered himself to be in good shape, but Sharon had him beat; wide shoulders and strong arms, tat sleeve from shoulder to wrist on her left arm. She winced as the medic touched a sensitive spot on the right side of her ribs, then caught Shook looking at her.

"Take a picture, Shook; it'll last longer," she said, making Park laugh and Thunder give a warning growl. Shook blushed and looked away as Park said, "Damn, Sharon. An oldie but a goodie. What DVD is that from again?"

"What's a DVD?" Sharon asked innocently. This time Shook laughed. "Ageism is an ugly thing, Sharon," Park said, then turned his attention back to Shook. "You did fuck up," he began, "But under the circumstances, I'd probably have done the same thing. That guy ran right when he saw us, and when you caught him, he started fighting. You called in the assistance call, though, and we got found, so it worked out."

"I guess," Shook said, kicking a rock or two at his feet.

"Plus," Park added, "We got to see Sharon get her ass kicked and how often does that happen? What with her hiding behind her dog and letting him fight her fights and....." But Park didn't finish because Sharon was off the bench in a flash, jacking his arm up behind his back. "Owwwwwwwwwwww.......shit!!" Park yelped.

"Say 'Aunt', Park," Sharon said. "Say it!!"

Thunder stayed seated on the bench, keeping a close eye on Sharon in case she needed some help. He yapped in the air twice, then lay his head on his paws. "Shit!! Gross!!" shouted the medic, holding her nose and waving a large gauze pad around Thunder's ass. "Get your dog out of my bus!" The medic yelled.

"Say it, Park!! Say 'aunt'." Park said it, so Sharon let him go. She slapped her thigh and Thunder hopped out of the ambulance and sat by her leg. She grabbed her vest and top off the ambulance door and got ready to walk back to her SUV. "Uh-uh," said Park. "Put your vest on."

"C'mon, Park. I'm just going to the car, then to the ER to get an x-ray. I'll have to take the vest off again anyway." Park just looked at her. She groused and slipped the vest back on, tightening the straps around her torso. "There, dad. Happy?"

"I'm not your dad. But if I was, I'd forbid you from getting any more tattoos."

She laughed and gave him the finger. Shook watched her walk away and asked, "'Say aunt?' What's that all about?"

"It's the female version of 'Say uncle', genius," Park responded.

"Oh, speaking of vests," Sharon said while walking backwards to the car, "Thunder's getting one soon. I'll shoot you a text when we put it on him. See ya." She opened the banged up rear door and Thunder jumped up in the SUV. She got behind the wheel and Park walked up and tapped on the glass. She rolled it down. "Text me when you're done at the ER to let me know what they say. And call your aunt to tell her you're ok."

"Ok, dad," she said quietly and drove away.

CHAPTER 12

Danny's phone buzzed in his shirt pocket while he was eating lunch in the break room. He put the tv on mute and answered, "Hey Cindy. Catch him already?"

"Almost," she said. "The phone's showing up at the nasty daddy strip club over on Hull St. You got any idea what kind of car he's driving? The lot's about halfway full. All Virginia plates. I was hoping we'd see a New York plate and we'd focus on that one. I think I'm going to send a guy in to see if he's in there."

"Make sure he's wearing a full body condom. I wouldn't go in there until a hazmat team had gone over the place. Twice. I'm not sure what kind of car he's currently driving. I would say something flashy, but that piece of shit he wrecked was halfway wrecked when he crashed it. So maybe he rolls low."

"Ok. No big deal. We've got photos of him, so we'll see if he's in there getting a lap dance from someone uglier than you," she said, then hung up.

* * *

"Ok," Cindy said. "Who wants to draw the short straw to go in and see if Defreitis is in there watching the dirty?" The two Marshals and one Richmond detective looked at each other, not saying anything. "Come on, boys. Make a decision. We're wasting time here." They all threw rock/paper/scissors and the Richmond detective lost. "Fuck," he cursed. He took off his gun, ammo magazines, and ballistic vest with *POLICE* emblazoned across the back and front. He kept his knife in his front pocket, but slipped it all the way into his pocket, so the slide clip wouldn't show. Luckily, most of the Fugitive guys dressed like they were a paycheck away from being homeless, so he didn't have to do much rearranging to fit in to the strip joint crowd.

"Remember," Cindy said. "Just see if he's in there, then shoot me a text. If he is in there, sit back and enjoy the show until he leaves, then give me a heads-up. We'll take him when he leaves the parking lot. If he's a shooter, I'd rather take him on a traffic stop away from a crowd." The detective nodded and got out of the Durango and walked over to the club.

A few minutes later she got a text:

he's her n the bak

What the fuck? She couldn't stand grown ass men texting like they were pre-teen boys. Then:

its drk in her i can't se too txt

Well, that made her feel a little better. Plus, if she was interpreting his first text correctly, he said that Defreitis was there and he was in the back. "He's in there guys," she told the Marshals. Then she called the non-emergency number for dispatch, officially called the Department of Emergency Communications. "Hey, it's 796. Look, we're out here at the nasty daddy on Hull Street. What? Haha, very funny. Yes, we're working. Anyway, we've got eyes on a fugitive in there. We're going to take him once he drives away. Can you send a MDT message to a unit or two and have them stage at St. Luke's Church just down the street? You can give them the cell number I'm calling you from and have them call me when they mark 10-23? What? No, I've never been to the buffet here."

Within minutes she heard 211 and 213 marking on scene at the church parking lot. Then her cell rang with an unfamiliar number. "Hello? Yeah, this is Cindy. Who's this? Who? Spell it. Never mind, too many letters. Are you guys set up? Ok, good. Once my guy tells me the target is coming out of the strip club, I'll get up on the radio with a description of the car he's driving and the direction he's going. My unit number is 796. Listen up for it on channel 2. What's your name again? Spell it again. Huh. The 'z' must be silent. Ok, listen up for us. 'Bye." The Marshal in the back seat asked, "What's the officer's last name?"

"Jones," she said. And they sat back to wait.

CHAPTER 13

Once Park and Shook got done processing their prisoner, they drove over to the Property and Evidence section to talk to Abad. He'd been involved in a shooting at the Fidelity Bank and shot and killed one of the bad guys. However, a civilian or two had complained to Internal Affairs that Abad froze up before he shot the guy, and while he was frozen a bank teller had gotten killed inside the bank. Another customer had also been shot and though he had survived, he was now blind. The second officer who was at the scene and had returned fire while in the rear parking lot had just recently resigned from the department. He had been cleared by Internal Affairs but decided cop work wasn't for him. Park didn't know what he was doing and really didn't care.

While IA was conducting their investigation, Abad had been stripped of his gun and badge, and placed on his current 'administrative' assignment. Park was initially hesitant to go by and see Abad, because he didn't want to make Abad self-conscious about not having his badge and gun while Park did. But after the initial visit, it wasn't awkward at all and Abad seemed to appreciate Park's concern. When Park and Shook walked into the P/E section, they found Abad at one of the desks, feet up and laptop in his lap. "You can't be looking at porn back here, Abad," Park joked. "What if IA has cameras down here that record you looking at 'Chicks with Dicks'?"

"Fuck them," Abad responded. "Porn's the only thing an Arabic cop can look at around here. Anything else and they think I'm plotting something. Speaking of porn, your people seem to have cornered the market on school girl stuff," referring to Park's Asian heritage. "I'd file a hostile work environment complaint against you if you weren't already sidelined," Park replied.

They bumped fists and Park sat on the edge of Abad's desk. "Lemons telling you anything?" Park asked, referring to the IA detective investigating Abad. "Are you kidding? That fucker isn't telling me shit. He's trying to hang my ass out to dry." Then, "Any word on if they found the second guy? Last I heard they thought he was from New York and had run back up there."

"I haven't heard anything else. Danny was helping the lead dick out on it, but he keeps getting pulled away for other shit. Hey, Shook?"

"What?" Shook was over at one of the desktop computers trying to log some of the prisoner's property into the system and having a hard time with it. "Never mind," sighed Park. Turning his attention back to Abad, he said, "Are you good to go for your hearing at city hall? Are you bringing a representative with you? Maybe an expert on use of force or active shooters?"

"Maybe," Abad said. "But I also might go the route Webb went and quit. I love being a cop. Or I did before this happened. Civilians or detectives who haven't worked the streets in years judging me and making decisions on something I did when they weren't there? It would be less of a headache and stress to do something else."

"Look, Abad," Park began. "I haven't been in your situation so I'm not going to tell you what you should or shouldn't do. I am going to tell you that I think you did your job and brought down a shooter. We already lost a good cop in Webb, and I wouldn't want to lose you, too. We need good, solid cops on the street. Cops like you."

"Thanks, Park. I'll see how it goes. No promises, though."

"Dammit, motherfucking piece of fucking shit!!!" Shook yelled, giving the finger to the desktop computer. "Fuck YOU!!!!!"

"I'd better go give your partner a hand before they jam him up too," Abad said, walking over to help Shook out. Park hoped Abad would fight the good fight and stay on with the department.

* * *

The rifle was still there. Hell, it looked like no one had even come in the house since he stashed it there months ago. Up in Brooklyn, if a house sat vacant for anytime at all it would either get taken over by squatters or worse, gentrifiers. In Maryland, just outside of Baltimore, however, the house was frozen in time. He pulled up the boards, used the same stick as last time and got rid of the spiderwebs, then pulled the gun out. He expanded the stock, dropped the magazine and cleared a round out of the chamber. Before Duane showed him, he would have had no idea how to do all this. Now Duane was gone, and Anthony started getting mad all over again. He was going to kill as many people as he could when he got to Richmond; starting with the first cop he could find.

CHAPTER 14

gt reddy. Hes comin out nw

Cindy read the text and got up on the radio, "796 to radio?"

"Go ahead, 796."

"Be advised the target may be getting ready to come out and get in his car. Stand-by and I'll give you the make, model, and plate when he gets in."

"10-4, 796. You want the air?"

"No need to hold the air right now, radio. We'll let you know more once we attempt the traffic stop."

Cindy and the Marshals watched from their unmarked SUV. Their target walked out the front door and over to a gold colored, full sized SUV with Virginia tags. She sent the detective inside the following text:

Just stay in there. We've got patrol guys with us. We'll come back and get you. Don't get chlamydia.

He texted back:

10-4. thats 1 of the stripers names

"Ok, guys get ready," she said. Then to the radio, "796, target is in a late model gold SUV, Virginia tags Lincoln, X-ray, King, 3245. Heading northbound on Hull St."

"Radio copies."

"211 and 213 copy," one of the patrol guys transmitted. "Want us to initiate?" he asked, meaning did Cindy want the patrol guys to initiate the traffic stop since they were in marked units. "10-4," she replied. "Whenever you're ready." Then she called Danny on his cell. "Hey Danny, we're getting ready to pull him over. Listen up on channel 2." She hung up without waiting on a reply. Both marked units passed her on the left and the lead unit hit his blue lights and bleeped his air horn once. Cindy saw the SUV's brake lights blink, then the front lift up as the driver accelerated. "211 to radio, he's not stopping," the officer said calmly. The pursuit was on.

* * *

Danny had been in his office typing up his running narrative when Cindy called to say that they'd spotted Defreitis coming out of the strip club. He shot her a text, asking her to make sure that Defreitis' vehicle was towed after he was caught. Danny wanted to get a search warrant for the vehicle, hoping to find something that would tie Defreitis to North 30th Street.

He turned his police radio on just when the tones went off about the vehicle not stopping when 211 tried to pull it over. He turned the volume up and called out for Taylor and Dean to come to his office and listen in.

"211, we're still northbound on Hull, speeds are close to sixty. Roads dry, traffic is light," Officer Juan Moreno transmitted. Whenever a pursuit began, a patrol supervisor began to monitor it. If speeds go too high, or there was a lot of traffic on the path, or it was a densely populated area, then the supervisor was required to terminate the pursuit. He or she could also terminate it if the underlying reason for the pursuit was a minor traffic infraction and/or if the driver was a known person. Finally, the pursuing officer could, and should, terminate the pursuit if conditions became too dangerous for all involved. Since Defreitis was wanted on an auto theft warrant and in connection with the *probable* murder of two people, Moreno had some leeway with the pursuit.

"211, we're coming up on the highway. If he gets on it, we're going to need to notify the state police. And.....disregard. He went under the overpass and is doing a U-turn...." Defreitis made a tight U-turn through the grassy median, followed by 211, 213, and Cindy's team in 796. Both

213 and Cindy weren't getting on the air, allowing Moreno to call it. If Moreno was having a hard time calling it and driving at the same time, then he would have told 213 to call it.

"211, we're coming up on Southside Plaza.... he's going to try and turn into the parking lot.......stand by....."

Defreitis tried to take the turn, but lost control of the SUV, the rear end sliding out into one of the supports holding up the *Welcome to Southside Plaza* sign. The SUV stopped with a jolt, airbag deploying in Defreitis' face. He muscled the door open and started running across the wide expanse of parking lot. 211 had overshot the turn and had to hop the median to U-turn back to the parking lot. "213 foot pursuit!!" Officer Ron Jones yelled as he pulled his SUV to a halt nearly parallel to Defreitis' SUV, jumping out and running after him. Defreitis had a decent head start on him, but Jones was gaining on him. Defreitis looked over his right shoulder and saw Jones gaining and tried to juke him by cutting to his left.......and ran right in to the side of Moreno's SUV as it cruised along beside him (*Why run when you can drive?* was Moreno's philosophy). Click-click went the handcuffs and Defreitis was in custody.

Cindy and her Marshals pulled up beside them as Moreno and Jones were searching Defreitis. "Awesome job, guys!!!" Cindy affirmed from the driver's seat of her SUV. She dialed Danny's number and said, "Patrol guys got him. We'll bring him to you in a few. Ok. 'Bye." Then to Moreno, "Put him the front seat beside me." She took a spare pair of cuffs from the center console and tossed them to Jones. "I'll tell the detective he's got your cuffs on him. You can use these until we get them back to you."

There was a loud, metallic creak coming from behind them. They all turned to look just as the *Welcome to Southside Plaza* sign collapsed slowly; first crunching Defreitis' SUV, then falling the rest of the way onto Jones' marked SUV. Defreitis and Jones both said "Fuck!" seconds apart. Cindy laughed as she pulled away.

CHAPTER 15

Danny asked Taylor to get the room ready for him while he gathered up the paperwork he'd need for the interview. In addition to the auto theft charge, they could now add an attempt to elude charge on Defreitis as well. Hopefully that would keep him in jail for a little longer and give Danny some time to build a case against him. Peck had texted him and said that she was still tied up in court but would head over to HQ when she was done to see if Defreitis was still talking to Danny. "Yo, Danny? It seems like all I do is set up this interview room for you," Taylor said. "It sure does seem that way to me, too. Why don't you ever catch a case? I need to talk to Dean about that," Danny retorted. "Never mind," Taylor grumbled as he got to work setting up the interview room.

Cindy and the Marshals came in a few minutes later; Defreitis looking a little dusty from the airbag and tackle, but overall not too bad. "You want him in 1 or 2?" Cindy asked, referring to the interview rooms. "2's fine," said Danny as he went to his fridge to grab a couple of waters. He walked into the interview room, gave a water to Defreitis, then stepped back out and pulled the door shut behind him. "He say anything on the way down?" Danny asked.

"Not really," Cindy answered. "Just that he wasn't too happy the sign fell on his SUV after he had wrecked it. Correction, the rental company's SUV. I guess he's worried about his deposit."

"Figures," Danny said. "He kills two people and's worried about a deposit on a rental." Then to Taylor, "Hey, can you run the plates and find out where that SUV was rented? We may have to take a ride to the rental company when we're done here."

"No problem," said Taylor. "How're you, Cindy? I like your hair that way."

"Thanks, Taylor. And stop flirting with me. I don't date cops."

Taylor grumbled a response and got digging on the SUV's plates.

* * *

"Ok, Mr. Defreitis, do you understand your rights?" Danny asked.

"Yeah, but why'm I down here?" Defreitis asked.

"Remember that car you wrecked awhile back? The one you had towed to that lady's yard? The owner reported it stolen."

"What??!! That's bullshit," Defreitis responded. "I've been driving that car around for months. I thought it belonged to my cousin Eddie Troy. I always rode around with him in the car. Shit, I paid for the insurance on that bitch. We'd go to 7-11 every month to get a money order for it. I didn't steal that car."

"Ever see the registration on it? To see who it belonged to?" Danny asked.

"No. Why would I? Eddie was always with it."

"Speaking of Eddie," Danny segued. "When's the last time you saw him?"

"Right before he disappeared. I went over to the house in Church Hill when I heard they were in town. I hugged both of them and borrowed their rental car for a few hours. When I left that evening, they were fine. When I was back up in New York, I heard that both of them were dead. It's all over Brooklyn."

In just that one statement, Defreitis had provided a plausible reason why his DNA would be at the house, in the car, and even on them. Danny asked him for a buccal (cheek) swab for a sample of his DNA which he provided readily.

"Where do you live?" Danny asked. "What state?"

"Man, I'm coast-to-coast," he responded. *Truly a drug dealer's life*, Danny thought.

"And why'd you have $1,300 dollars on you when you were arrested?" Danny asked.

"Is it illegal to have money?" Defreitis asked. "I don't trust banks," he said. "Anything else, detective?" Being a smartass now.

"Nope," said Danny. "I'm going to get a search warrant for that SUV you were driving and take a real good look at the clothes you had in the back seat. That bag? When you wrecked, some of them spilled out of the bag and it looked like a pair of jeans had some blood on them."

For the first time in the interview, Defreitis appeared nervous, but then composed himself quickly. "Whatever, man. I want my lawyer now."

"Yeah, I thought you would," Danny said, leaving the room.

"I got the license plate information back," Taylor offered, as Danny came into the observation room. Peck was already in there taking notes. Danny said hi to her and motioned for Taylor to continue.

"It was rented out of Jacksonville Airport, luckily with a credit card. The gal's name is Nicole White and she's in the Navy. I made a few calls to the NCIS and they're going to bring her in and see what she has to say."

"That's great, Taylor. Thanks." Then to Peck, "How long do you think we can hold him?"

"I can try to make sure he doesn't get a bond. Trial should be in about a month. We'll probably have to dump the auto theft charge. I'm sure the owner let him and Troy use the car. We'd lose that one. On the attempt to elude, since no one was hurt, he'd just have to pay a fine. So, bottom line, you've got a little less than a month if you want to charge this guy."

"Great. Just fucking great," whined Danny, walking out of the room.

CHAPTER 16

Shook had Park drop him off on the ground floor of HQ so he could walk up the six flights to get his steps in; yes, he was *that* guy. He came out of the stairwell onto the 3rd floor where the Major Crimes offices were. Danny was waiting for him, leaning over the reception desk, typing on his phone. "Hey, detective," greeted Shook.

"It's 'Danny'. How're you doing, Shook? Thrilled to be back here, right?" Shook had been assigned to Danny for a few days the past year, listening to jail calls and running some things down. It was productive work and got results, but by the end of it, Shook had decided patrol life was for him.

Shook hemmed and hawed for a few seconds before Danny let him off the hook. "Just kidding, Shook. I know it sucks. But I also know that even though you don't like it, you stick to it and that's what I need. You were at the house on 30th Street and saw the blood. Has Park been keeping you up to date on what's going on?"

"He's told me some things. Mainly that it's probably going to be a double murder over drugs."

"That's the gist of it. We've got the guy in custody, but he'll be released in a month unless we find more charges against him or can prove the murders. Which is why I need you to listen to jail calls again. He just got locked up, so it's much less than the last round you did for me." Shook had listened to nearly a hundred jail calls a few months ago in reference to a murder in Byrd Park.

"I'm writing a search warrant for the guy's SUV. Once I get done with that and make a few calls, you should be done with the jail calls. You can roll over with me to serve the search warrant and help with processing the car if you want," Danny offered. Shook agreed and Danny set him up in the same vacant office he had used last time. Danny gave him the CD with the jail calls on it and Shook was relieved to see it only had 8 calls. Shook plugged in his headphones and got to listening.

CHAPTER 17

"I don't like doing this, Sharon," Officer Carl Bailey, unit #115, said.

"You're such a wuss," Officer Kim Byrd, unit #119, replied.

"'Wuss'?" Sharon Wright mocked. "I can't remember the last time I heard that word, except when my parents were trying to talk 'cool' back in the day." Thunder lay on the floor of the vacant house, head on paws, watching the three talk. He was getting bored and wanted to get to work.

"I'm bringing the word back to us millennials. Join the wuss revolution," Byrd replied.

"I still don't want to do this," Bailey repeated.

"Look, Carl," Sharon began. "I need to get Thunder back to where he's comfortable searching houses again." Thunder had sustained a major injury last year but had made a full recovery. Since his injury, he hadn't had an opportunity to search a house and Sharon wanted to knock the rust off of him. Plus, he'd just gotten fitted for his ballistic vest and she wanted to run him through some paces while wearing it to get him used to the additional weight.

"Ok, but why do I have to hide in the closet? Why can't Kim?" Bailey complained.

"Because I've got seniority," Byrd answered.

"We were in the same academy class!! Your code is only 3 lower than mine." City employees were issued a numerical code when they're hired; the lower the code, the more senior the employee.

"Right. So, I'm senior. Get in the closet," Byrd directed.

"Dammit," Bailey cursed as he stepped inside the cramped space. "It stinks in here, too," he added as Byrd closed the door on him.

"Now listen, Carl," Sharon said. "When he finds you, he's going to paw, bark, and scratch at the door. Whatever you do, DON'T open it until I tell you to. And when you do, cover your balls with both hands. Just in case."

"He could cover his balls with one hand," Byrd added.

"Fuck *THAT*!" Carl said and walked out of the closet. Byrd pushed him back in and closed the door again.

"Thunder and I are going to go outside for a second. When we do, go hide in another closet. Got it?"

"If you want me to move to another closet, why'd I get in this one in the first place?" Bailey asked reasonably.

"Because it's funny," Byrd said, and she and Sharon laughed. Thunder's tail thumped three times, joining in the mirth.

"Fine. Whatever," Bailey said. "C'mon, Kim, let's go," Sharon said, leaving Bailey to find somewhere else to hide.

* * *

"113 to radio? Mark me 10-7 on a meal."

"10-4, 113. 1225hrs," the dispatcher relayed to Park. He pulled up into the parking lot of the Mexican place right off the downtown expressway that had the best burritos around. He was concerned at first because there were three VSP (Virginia State Police) cars backed into spots at the restaurant. Park didn't like eating somewhere where there were already two or more police cars; it looked bad, like the cops were just hanging out. That was ok at precincts, but gave the wrong impression in public.

The crisis was averted, though, as the three troopers came out to their car, nodding at Park as they passed. All three troopers were trim and appeared to be in excellent shape. Shoes shiny, uniforms ironed to nearly razor-sharp creases, and campaign hat angled just so on their shaved heads. Some city cops Park knew thought troopers were assholes, but Park knew that they carried themselves that way for a reason. The intimidating persona contributed to officer safety. Troopers, like most of the cops in the city and surrounding jurisdictions, rode solo and very often did not notify their dispatcher when they were out on traffic stops. When you're by yourself on the highway, you need to command respect to lessen your chances of being assaulted. If a city officer gets in a fight, his or her back is usually less than a minute away. A trooper's back up could be MILES away.

Regardless, as Park passed them, he sucked his gut in a bit, then let it back out once he'd gone by. As he opened the door to the restaurant, he heard an airhorn toot and saw Danny driving into the parking lot. Danny backed into a space next to Park's car and jogged up to him at the door.

"You didn't have to jog, Danny. I'd have waited for you."

Danny slowed to a walk, poked Park under his vest with his finger, and said, "Just showing you what a jog looks like, Park," then went inside. Park followed silently, then kicked Danny's foot mid-step, making him stumble against a table, banging his elbow. "Whoops," Park said, then got in front of Danny to order lunch.

"What the hell, Sharon??!!" Bailey asked, looking a smidge pale. There was a small tear in the front of his pants where Thunder had nipped at him. It didn't break his skin, but it did put a small hole in his pants. He'd decided to go a floor down and hide in a closet in the kitchen. He heard Sharon yell, "Richmond Police! Come out or I release the dog!!" She said it two more times and then he heard Thunder's feet on the wood floors. It took him all of about 45 seconds to find Bailey. Bailey sprang out of the closet and yelled at Thunder at the top of his lungs. Which was when Thunder perforated his pants.

"I told you he's a little rusty," Sharon answered.

"I hope you're wearing underwear, Carl. If not, I'm filing some kind of complaint," Byrd warned.

"Yeah, whatever. I know you were looking when they cut off my clothes after I got shot last year," Bailey said. It was a close call, the shooting, but Bailey had made a full recovery.

"I did look and thought you'd just gotten out of a cold pool," Byrd said, "Then rolled around in the snow," she added.

"Did he get you?" Sharon asked. Not necessarily out of concern for Bailey; she just didn't want to have to do the ton of paperwork for an accidental bite.

"No, I'm fine. And he did a pretty good job of finding me. Didn't you boy?" looking at Thunder. Thunder thumped his tail, agreeing with Bailey's assessment. "C'mere," Bailey said to him. Bailey got down on a knee and Thunder walked over for a hug, his new vest still a little stiff. Thunder and Bailey had been injured about the same time and visited each other while convalescing. Ordinarily, only a K9 officer and maybe their immediate family would hug a working dog. But Thunder made an exception for Bailey.

"Ok, enough of this cuddly shit," said Byrd. "Let's mark 10-8 and get back to work." Bailey gave Thunder a quick kiss on the snout and got back to work.

* * *

Danny was still rubbing his elbow as he and Park sat down to eat. Neither liked having their back to a door, so they each took a small table. Danny needed the room for his portable radio, cell phone, and glasses. Back in the day, Park could have used the room for five tacos, a large drink, and a side of chips and salsa. Today, his table looked pathetic with one 'skinny' burrito and a side of salsa, hold the chips.

"I could have broken my arm, Park. Tripping me up around all hard surfaces." Park shrugged and looked around for some hot sauce. Danny handed him a bottle that was on his table and Park grunted a thanks. "Anyway, how's Sharon? That guy got her a couple good ones in the gut, I heard."

"She's ok. Tough kid. Does all the CrossFit, weights. I'm sure her pride hurts worse than her gut. Speaking of hurt pride, how's Shook doing?"

Danny got the sauce back from Park and shook some on each of his three tacos. And a little on his chips. With a splash in his salsa. *Should have tripped him twice*, Park thought, looking at the spread compared to his. "He's doing ok, I guess. I was going to bring him to lunch with us, but he had a few more calls to get through, and.......hold up." Danny's phone was vibrating on the table. "Speak of the devil.....hello? What's up, Shook?"

Park eyed a chip as Danny listened. Danny saw him do it and slid the basket over to him. Park slid it back. "Uh-huh. He said that? Can you hear it clearly?......."

Danny slid the basket over to Park again. Park pushed it back, harder this time, dislodging a chip. "Ok. Sounds good. I'll be back in about 30. Want me to bring you anything?...At the Mexican place off the expressway.......How many tacos? Damn. Ok. Loaded? Ok. See you soon."

"What happened to the chip that fell out of the basket?" Danny asked. "Dunno," said Park, wiping his mouth. "What'd Shook say?"

"The next to last call. 'Penultimate.' Like that? Detective shit." Park made an up and down, hurry-the-fuck-up gesture with his hand. "Anyway, the guy says, *'They don't even know they're dead yet.'* A brain surgeon, he ain't." Danny balled up his taco wrappers and tossed them in with the chips he didn't eat. "So, after I pick up six tacos for Shook, I'm going to go over and give a listen to that call. Then take him with me over to search the car. You good?"

"Yeah. I'm going to sit in here and finish my burrito in peace, enjoy the fact that you're gone."

"Yeah, right, Park. You wouldn't know how to act without me," Danny said as he went to get in line for more tacos.

CHAPTER 18

"So, he says that shit on the next to last call?" Danny asked Shook as he walked into the office. "Yep," confirmed Shook. "So, he knows they're dead. And......."

"Yesssss.......," Danny waited.

"He says that the detective who interviewed him has, and I quote, 'a stick up his ass,' unquote." Danny laughed and told Shook to play the part about *not knowing they're dead* again.

Once he heard it a few times, he told Shook to copy that file and email it over to Peck in the prosecutor's office. "Get my lunch?" Shook asked. "It's in the break room. Come find me when you're done, and we'll head over to the police tow lot to look through the car with Forensics." Danny headed back to his office to make a few calls and kill some time while Shook ate.

* * *

"You ever get a chance to do any search warrants yet?" Danny asked Shook on the drive over.

"You mean getting the warrants or executing them?" Shook responded.

"Either, or," Danny answered. "When I was in patrol, I didn't do much drug stuff, so I never got the chance. Once I transferred up to Major Crimes, I started doing tons of them."

"I've never written one, but I've been there on a few entries when Narcotics was serving them," Shook responded.

"I'll email you some sample ones that you can keep on your computer drive. They'll come in handy whether you stay in patrol or transfer out to another unit. Then... hold up a second. Let me go talk to this guy real quick." Danny hit his rear deck lights and stopped beside a median to talk to a guy holding a sign that said, "USMC veteran. Anything would help." It looked like the guy had made the sign out of an old pizza box.

"I've seen this guy all over the place," Shook said. "I think he's a little 10-96 (cop talk for mentally unstable)."

"Probably," Danny said, stepping out of the car. "He used to be a cop."

* * *

"Unit 113 log, unit to back, respond to the 14th Street Bridge, center of the span, for a report of a person standing on the ledge. Unit taking the back advise, respond code 1."

Before Park could respond, Officer Percy Smith answered up, "117, I've got his back. Responding from the Bottom." Meaning Percy was responding from the Shockoe Bottom area of the city.

"And 113 copies from 14th and Broad," Park answered. Both he and Percy were coming from about the same distance; he was at the far east end of downtown and Percy from Shockoe Bottom. The 'Bottom' was a valley between downtown and Church Hill, well known for clubs and festivals. It had been an area full of tobacco warehouses until they shut down and were abandoned. Developers came in and turned them into apartments. Very expensive apartments. Like much of Richmond, the area was booming.

As Park turned onto 14th St, he saw Percy's SUV a few blocks ahead of him. He got in behind him and both marked on scene minutes later. Park turned on his rear deck lights and hit the switch that sends a blue light arrow to the left, indicating that people needed to switch lanes because this one was blocked.

"What's up, P?" Park asked, walking up to Percy.

"Not much, Twin. Ready to go see what's cooking up here?" Percy and Park resembled each other in height and weight while they were in the academy, so they'd refer to each other as twins. "Yeah, let's go up and take a look. Between this bridge and the Lee Bridge, it's jumper central."

A growing crowd of people was on the sidewalk near where the person was balancing on the 4' wall that ran the length of the bridge. A few other cars had slowed down when they came abreast of the jumper, then moved on once they realized not much was going on. "Come on folks, move on, move on. Get out of the way, please back up," Percy directed, as he waded through the crowd. Once Park and Percy made it to the front of the crowd, they saw a woman with her back to them, standing on the other side of the protective wall. The ledge she was standing on extended about 2' out, so she wasn't necessarily in danger of falling off a narrow ledge. Unless she got dizzy from heights and just tumbled off before she could jump. It was 100' down to the surface of the James River. The summer drought had lowered the surface of the river and large rocks showed through the surface.

People, of course, had their cameras out, taking video and pictures of the situation; most hoping for some disaster they could post somewhere online. "Ma'am?" Percy said. "Ma'am? My name is Percy. I'm with the police department. This is my partner, Park. What's going on today? Why are you up here?"

Since Percy was the first one to talk to her, he was the primary negotiator. If he built a rapport with her, he would continue to talk to her to try to get her off the ledge. Park looked over the wall and saw the fire department's water rescue boat making its way down the river to the bridge. They'd hang out a bit upriver and come in if she jumped.

They made sure to not get underneath her since a human body plummeting from 100' could kill one or more firefighters on the boat.

Park was getting ready to get on the radio to see if negotiators were on the way when the woman turned to face them, the officers seeing the baby in her arms for the first time.

CHAPTER 19

"How're you doing, Officer Wassmer?" Danny asked, stepping up to the man in the median strip. Shook had gotten out of the car as well and was standing in front of the unmarked, keeping an eye on the traffic behind them and blading his gun side away from the homeless guy in the median. "116 to radio?" Shook said. "Go ahead, 116," came the reply. "Det. Jacobs and I will be out with an individual in the median, 1300 block of Brook Rd. We're 10-4."

"Radio copies."

Wassmer looked at Shook's stance, then turned his attention back to Danny.

"New guy?" Wassmer asked.

"Yup," Danny replied.

"Good tactics," Wassmer observed. "Gun side bladed away from me, keeping his eye out for traffic but keeping me in his peripheral, calling in his location. All good stuff."

"Yeah, Officer Wassmer. You taught his FTO's FTO, so your training is still getting passed down from generation to generation." An FTO is a Field Training Officer. "Anyway,"

Danny continued, "How are you doing? You ok for money and food? Got some place to lay your head?"

"I was a cop and a US Marine, Jacobs. I'm always ok," Wassmer replied. But he didn't look it. He was skinny and sickly looking. He was wearing his Marine cap, a red t-shirt, and tan cargo pants. All looked dirty and threadbare. From time to time, Wassmer would cock his head to the side and listen to the voices in his head, nod, then refocus on Danny.

Danny knew better than to ask him a second time if he needed anything. Wassmer still had his pride and refused to take anything from cops. Danny had asked him a second time the first time he saw him on the street and Wassmer cursed him up and down and turned his back on him. He wouldn't acknowledge Danny for months afterward. Danny saw a marked SUV coming down the street towards them. It tooted its air horn twice and a hand waved out the window, followed by, "Hey Officer Wassmer!" Then the SUV rolled on down the road.

"Ok, we're going to go ahead and shove off," Danny said. "Shook there and I need to search a car. Hopefully get something to put a murderer away for a long time."

"Take it easy, Jacobs. Watch your six, rookie," Wassmer said, then walked over to a car that had stopped to give him a dollar bill.

Danny and Shook got back in the car and Shook cleared up on the radio. "Did that guy teach at the academy when you went through?" Shook asked.

"Yep," said Danny, checking the side mirror as he changed lanes. "He taught officer safety and defensive tactics. Always wore short shorts and socks pulled up to his knees. Hell of an instructor, though."

"What happened to him?" Shook asked. "Did he do his full 25yrs and get his pension?"

"Nope. I think he did around 16, then quit to follow some woman down to Florida. I heard he joined up with a PD down there, then the woman dumped him. That pushed him over the edge, and he started hearing voices. He got jammed up on the department and came back up here."

Shook looked in his side mirror; Wassmer getting smaller as they drove further away. "He says he was an ex-Marine. Does he ever tell people he used to be a cop?" Shook asked.

"He did when he first started begging. Then one day he got beat up real bad by a bunch of drones who had nothing better to do than hurt a defenseless man. Just because he used to be a cop." Danny's knuckles turned white on the steering wheel at the memory. Wassmer disappeared from the mirror as they turned the next corner. They drove in silence the rest of the way to the tow lot.

* * *

It was starting to get hot out on the bridge. Summertime in Richmond, no shade, Kevlar vests, dark blue uniforms made mainly of polyester. Not to mention two officers who weighed in at over 220lbs a piece. Every so often a medic would come over and hand Park a couple of waters. He'd give one to Percy who'd then offer it to Mary (it had taken Percy a solid 10 minutes of talking before he got her name out of her), who'd refuse. To be honest, Park couldn't care less about Mary. She'd been selfish enough to bring an infant with her on the ledge. As far as he was concerned, she was dead to him. He was sure Percy felt the same way (and all the other first responders as well). But Percy was a pro and kept his feelings in check.

"Mary," Percy said, "That baby need some water, apple juice, or something. He's going to get dehydrated. Or she. Boy or girl, Mary?"

"She's a girl," Mary said quietly, pulling the swaddling back just a bit to look into her face. "My miracle baby."

"Why's she your miracle baby, Mary? Did it take you awhile to have her? Did you have to go to a fertility doctor? My wife and I did, too. We've got a miracle baby. It took so long, but we got him. A son. Just like your daughter."

Mary didn't say anything. Just kept looking at her daughter, tears streaming down her face. "Please, Mary. Just take one of these water bottles for your baby. Look, I'll leave it right here and walk away from it. You can walk over and get it." Percy left the bottle on the top of the bridge rail and backed away from it. Mary inched toward it, picked it up, and then went back to where she was standing. She held the bottle in her hand, then dropped it into the river. *Bitch.*

Danny and Shook got to the tow lot less than 10 minutes after speaking with Wassmer. "Go ahead and serve the warrant, Shook, then we can get to looking. It's hot as fuck and I don't want to be out here for hours." Shook agreed and put his name, code number, date, time, and the Sheriff's name on the back of the warrant. (Serving a warrant is also called 'backing' it, since the back is where the serving officer signs it.)

A Forensic unmarked Impala pulled into the lot a few minutes later and Sydney squared got out; two Forensic investigators, both named Sydney, but one spelled Sidney. When they worked together, to avoid confusion, they'd sometimes be referred to as "with a y or with an i," such as, "Hey, 'with an i? Did you get that shell casing?" The detectives thought it was funnier than Sydney squared did. The Richmond PD used a combination of sworn detectives and civilians to fill the ranks of the Forensic Unit. Sydney squared were both civilians and as such could not serve search warrants; only sworn officers/detectives could. Sydney Kline got out of the car and walked over to Danny. "We're all set, Danny. Looking for anything with blood on it, right?"

"Yep. Hopefully a gun, too. But this guy is 'coast-to-coast,' so I take it to mean he's got some experience in the drugs/gun game. I bet he tossed it somewhere along I-95." Kline rolled her eyes at the coast-to-coast reference and went to help Sidney Banks grab their equipment.

Danny and Shook stood by while Sydney (with a 'y') started taking their pictures and documenting observations about the car. That completed, they opened the car up and heat waves rolled out of it.

"Goddamn, Danny. You couldn't pick a hotter day to do this, could you?" Sidney (with an 'i') asked.

"You guys want to step on it? The ice in my coffee is starting to melt," Danny joked. Banks gave him the finger and went back to work. Kline had found a suitcase in the rear of the car and opened it. She was spreading the clothes out on a sterile sheet she had put on the ground when Danny's cell phone rang. He looked at the caller ID and saw it was from a New York area code.

"Det. Jacobs. Yeah. Who? Det. Bartlett? Oh, Barrett. What's up? Yeah......uh-huh......how many? In the trunk?.......Ok. How long?........You guys are processing it now? Ok. Yeah, thanks. I'll call you soon." Danny hung up and Shook asked, "That NYPD?"

"Yeah. They found them in the trunk of that rental car, parked a few blocks from Troy's house in Brooklyn."

Kline was taking pictures of a pair of pants she had found in the suitcase. "What'd you find Sydney?" Danny asked.

"Blood."

Traffic in Alexandria, Virginia was a straight bitch! He was doing fine all the way through Maryland and into DC, but once he hit the Virginia line, Anthony had slowed to a virtual crawl. And he was starting to get a little paranoid. He wondered of they'd found the driver's body yet. Surely by now someone would have noticed the driver missing, right? Did the driver service have a dispatch center like the cab companies? Was anyone looking for the guy? Had the car been reported stolen? So many questions bouncing around in his head. The rifle was on the passenger side floorboard with a hoodie covering most of it. Looking over at it calmed him down, comforted him. If he got pulled over, he was going to grab it off the floor and come out shooting. He was going to be famous.

CHAPTER 20

Sharon had pulled up to the scene on the bridge and she and Thunder walked over to where Park was standing. She had a collapsible water dish in her cargo pants pocket and put it on the ground. A medic tossed her a bottle of water and she filled up Thunder's bowl. He sniffed it once, then lapped it up.

"So, what's the deal with this lady?" she asked Park. "I heard the call come in while we were at the kennels, so I figured I'd come over and see if you and Percy needed a hand."

"I'm not sure what her deal is, but she's got a fucking baby in her arms and won't give her any water," Park answered. "Percy's been talking to her for about 45minutes. She talked to him initially, but now she just stares at the baby, then down at the rocks."

They both watched as Percy kept trying to get Mary to say something to him.

"Want me to go over there and try?" Sharon asked. "Maybe a woman-to-woman, thing?"

"Hey, P?" Park called. Percy looked over and saw Sharon standing next to Park. Park pointed at Sharon, then at Mary and shrugged his shoulders. Percy nodded and walked over to them, telling Mary that he'd be right back. "Hey, baby girl," Percy said to Sharon as he came over. Percy and her father were the only people allowed to call her that. "You want to give it a shot? She talked to me at first, then she shut down after she threw a bottle of water into the river. All I know is that her name is Mary, the baby is a girl, and she calls her a 'miracle baby.'"

"Sure, I'll go over there and talk to her. No negotiators?" she asked.

"They're tied up on some kind of barricade situation over in the west end. They would have sent someone, but we initially had good rapport, so we told them to take care of their business over there. I was on the team for years, so they were cool with it," Percy answered.

"Ok. Let's see how it goes," Sharon said. She gave Thunder the command to stay and walked over to talk to Mary. Park, Percy, and Thunder, the three males who meant the most to her, watched her go.

* * *

"How much blood?" Danny asked. He'd made a note of the NYPD detective's name and number, then walked back over to where Sydney squared were.

"You can see some here," Kline pointed out at the inside of the waist band. "And maybe some around the cuffs of the pants," she said. "And..........looks like some bleach spots on the pants cuffs, too." Indicating an attempt to clean up a crime scene. "Like maybe he splashed it on his pants leg," offered Banks. "You know it's blood for sure?" Danny asked.

"Pretty sure," Sydney said. "We'll test it once we get back to HQ. It would be nice if it matched one or both of our vics."

She started packing it up to take back to the lab at HQ. "What'd the guy from New York say?" Banks asked.

"They got a call about something leaking from a car's trunk up in Brooklyn. The patrol guys got there and saw what looked like black paint on the ground at the rear of the car."

"I bet it didn't smell like paint," said Sydney as she was taping up the bag.

"Bingo," Danny said. "They took one whiff and knew it was some kind of body. Human or animal. They popped open the trunk and found both of them in there; one on top of the other one. Looked like they'd been shot, but they'd melted some. They're on the way to the Medical Examiner's office."

"You going up there?" Sidney asked, hoping for a road trip to NYC. "Maybe," Danny replied. "Depends on what Peck says. If we take the bodies, we'll have to figure out some way to get their evidence. If they take them, same issue. We'll see."

"Ok, we're all done here. You going to take the search warrant over to the courthouse and file it?" Sydney asked. "You bet. C'mon Shook. Let's roll. Thanks 'with an i' and 'with a y'," Danny said, getting four middle fingers in return.

CHAPTER 21

"Mary, you need to give that baby some water. She's got to be parched. It's so hot out here. Please? Just give her a little bit," Sharon said. Mary was really starting to get on her nerves. She'd been talking to her for the last 15 minutes and still hadn't gotten much out of her. She turned to Park and Percy to get some ideas from them, when she got a sharp pain in her side from the fight the other day.

Mary saw her wince and asked, "What happened to you?"

"I got hurt at work the other day," Sharon replied. Then an idea came to her. "A man did it," she added.

Mary started nodding her head, rocking the child back and forth. "I know how a man can hurt you," Mary said. "Hurt every inch of you. Inside and out."

Sharon stayed silent, nodding her head at Mary, urging her to continue. But Mary got silent again. Just nodding and looking at her daughter, swaddled in a thin blanket.

"Is that what happened to you, Mary? Did a man hurt you? Is that why you're out here?" Sharon asked. "Let me help you," Sharon continued. "We can get this guy locked up. Put the asshole in jail. We can do it. You can do it."

"This man," Mary began, "He hurt me two years ago. I was walking home from the library on Westbrook Ave. Near Brook Road? I walked home all the time. I loved that library. Then that man came. That man hurt me."

Sharon was listening, but she noticed something odd about the baby; she hadn't heard her crying recently. How long had it been since she'd heard the cry?

"I was cutting through the alley over to my house on East Seminary. It was still daylight. Still broad daylight."

Thunder was the first to sense the change in Sharon's body language. He alerted and sat up, cocking his head to look at her sideways.

"I can't remember what book I checked out that day. I tried to read one a week. That library always had the best books."

Sharon stared at the baby in Mary's arms to see if she could detect any movement at all. She inched closer to Mary.

"I was walking by an old garage. I can still smell how that alley smelled. Like trash and dust. Some overgrown weeds near the garage. The door cracked open. I didn't really pay it any mind."

Thunder started padding at the ground, a low growl in his throat. Park and Percy noticed and began walking toward Sharon.

"When he grabbed me I tried to scream, but he put his hand over my mouth and pulled me into the garage. My leg got cut on the aluminum frame. He punched me in the face. Over and over. I tasted blood in my mouth and couldn't breathe. He pulled my pants down, then my underwear."

Sharon saw a limp hand fall from the swaddling. A little, limp arm.

"He forced himself inside of me. It hurt so bad. He choked me as he was hurting me. I can still feel him hurting me. Can smell him. I'll never forget that smell. Never."

"Mary! Hand me that baby now!!" Sharon said. Taking more steps toward her.

"After he was done, he hit me again. Called me a slut. Said I was asking for it. Dressing like that. I was wearing a t-shirt and pants. That's all. I wasn't asking for it."

Thunder started barking. Park and Percy started moving faster toward Sharon.

"Nine months later I had her. I had my daughter. My miracle baby. Today I smelled him again. I felt him again. He's going to hurt me again. He's going to hurt my baby again."

"Mary, NO!!" Sharon lunged over the railing just as Mary jumped, baby in her arms, and fell 100' to the rocks below. Park and Percy both grabbed Sharon's duty belt just before she toppled over after Mary, Thunder's barking nearly deafening everyone. The only thing louder was Sharon's bellow of rage.

* * *

News crews were on the bridge, doing their remotes with the downtown skyline in the background. Dusk was coming, and the buildings had their office lights on, a nice urban look.

The fire department had motored slowly away from the scene after getting Mary's and her baby's bodies off the rocks. They'd done their best to wash the blood from the rocks, but they'd have to get a truck on the bridge and shoot a spray of water down. It was decided to let the river do the work when the water rose. Now it was a gory image the networks could use on their reports if they chose to do so; if it bleeds, it leads.

H/R Removal Service had arrived, packed up the bodies for transport, and would take them the to the Medical Examiner's Office for an autopsy. They gently placed the little body bag containing Mary's baby on top of her body bag. Park thought it awful that they made body bags so small.

Sharon had both arms on the bridge wall's parapet and was looking down at the water below; Thunder right beside her, facing the opposite direction guarding her six. Park got done talking to Percy, shook his hand and walked over to Sharon. Thunder saw him coming and thumped his tail twice. Park nudged him over and leaned on the railing beside Sharon.

"The kid was already dead, wasn't she?" Sharon asked.

"Yeah," confirmed Park. "The medical examiner who responded out here thought she'd been dead for a day or two. Percy and I were just talking about it and both realized we never heard a word from the baby. We just caught glimpses of her head when Mary would move from time to time."

Thunder nuzzled Sharon's leg and she reached down and scratched behind his ears.

"I pulled her up on the MDT to see what the deal was with her rape. Awful. Stranger rape. It doesn't look like she had any idea who this guy was. They caught him a few weeks later when he tried to grab another woman. Picked the wrong one; she had a CCW (Carry Concealed Weapon permit) and shot him twice. First shot was in the balls. Second in the face; after about five minutes, hopefully."

"Good," said Sharon. "I hope he rots in hell."

Thunder gave a small chuff in agreement.

"I wonder why she thought she smelled him?" Sharon asked.

"Maybe she got a whiff of a smell that reminded her of him. Or maybe her baby dying brought back memories of him. Or maybe none of the above. Wondering will drive you crazy."

"I guess," said Sharon, still scratching Thunder behind the ears.

"You ready to go, kiddo? It's almost EOT time," Park said.

"I'm going to stay here for a little while longer, enjoy the breeze and the city lights."

"Ok," Park said, giving her back a rub, feeling the Kevlar vest under her uniform shirt. "Hold up," she said as he turned to walk away. He looked at her and saw tears forming in her eyes. "Could you stay with me for few minutes, Dad? Please." Then put her hand to her mouth to hold in the sob.

Park walked back over and leaned against her as they looked at their city, Thunder squeezed between them, head on paws. She put her head on her dad's shoulder and watched the river flow.

* * *

Anthony had finally broken free of all the traffic and had gotten as far as Fredericksburg, when the sun started to go down. He was tired as fuck. Between the recent sleepless nights and the fucked-up traffic, he was exhausted. Richmond was only about an hour south of here, so he pulled off the highway and started looking for some vacant store with a large parking lot. The exit ramp took him out to Route 1 and one thing that was constant all along Route 1 was vacant businesses. It seemed like whichever state he was in, somewhere on that north-south stretch of road, there was a vacant store with a large parking lot. And sure enough, there was an old K-Mart store not even two blocks south of the exit. He pulled into the lot, circled it once and then backed into one of the loading dock spots in the back. He turned the car all the way off, put on the hoodie that had been hiding his rifle, then tilted the seat back. He moved the rifle over to his lap and closed his eyes. He wasn't worried about falling asleep tonight; the crunching sound of the knife going into the guy's skull was all the lullaby he needed.

CHAPTER 22

The next morning Danny was working on his own again; Shook had grown bored of the detective lifestyle, again, and went back to ride with Park. Danny couldn't blame him; many times, he felt the same way. He'd been in Patrol for nearly a decade before moving over to Major Crimes. He always enjoyed patrol work and felt the camaraderie between patrol officers was unrivaled. From time to time, he'd get the itch to go back to patrol work.

But now he had work to do on the double. He'd spoken with his NYPD liaison and the bosses up there were hesitant to claim the bodies as their murders. After all, they concluded, the couple was probably killed in Richmond and transported to New York to be dumped. Richmond bosses, on the other hand, felt the same way and posited that even if they were shot in Richmond, they may not have died until they were in NYC or anywhere in between. RVA brass knew they couldn't drag DC, MD, DE, and NJ into it, but thought NY could take it.

Herein lay the problem with detective work that generally didn't affect patrol work; politics. Not the Democrat/Republican kind. The numbers kind. Cities simply did not want to add numbers to their homicide count. Or any crimes for that matter. Danny didn't pretend to understand the reasoning behind it, nor did he care. It was his job to solve the cases and that's what he tried his best to do. He saw that he had a message on his landline's voice mail. He punched in his code and heard the following:

"This message is for Detective Jacobs. I got your name and number from the story in yesterday's paper. I've got some information on those people from New Jersey who got killed. Call me at the number on your caller ID."

Danny called the number.

* * *

Sharon squatted down, getting a good grip on the Olympic bar. She had used liquid chalk on her hands for some additional grip. She never wore gloves because her hands were already rough from the training, but it was a Richmond summer and she was sweating her ass off. This was her last clean and jerk, so she wanted to make sure it didn't slip out of her hands. She took two deep breaths and then heaved it up into the air, bracing herself, then lowering it. She never slammed weights; like Park always told her: if you can't lower it, don't lift it.

She worked her neck from side to side and took a drink of water. A few summers ago, she hadn't stayed hydrated one workout and wound up going to the ER in an ambulance. She thought sure she was having a heart attack. $1,500 later, she discovered it was a powerful muscle contraction brought on by dehydration. Lesson learned.

She was working out in the backyard of her smallish house in the northside of Richmond. Her yard was green for the most part, except where she did her workouts. Tractor tires, rusty sledge hammers, beat-up plyo boxes, pleather heavy bag, and a couple cinder blocks for grip work. And obviously, the 40lb Olympic bar with bumper plates. There was similar equipment at each of the four precincts, but she preferred to workout at home. Plus, she let Thunder out of his kennel while she worked out, so he enjoyed it as well. Currently he was chewing on an old car tire, dragging it around the yard as the shade shifted during the morning. Sharon was probably anthropomorphizing, but she thought he was probably embarrassed that he got injured so badly a year ago and wanted to make sure it wouldn't happen again. Right after it happened, the vet didn't think he could recover enough to go back to police work. But Thunder wasn't ready to retire, so he rehabbed like a motherfucker and got back to 100 percent.

She was covered in sweat and feeling a comfortable burn along her thighs, ass, and shoulders. She'd get an occasional twinge in her side where that guy got her, but it was getting better daily. She was getting ready to go in and hit the shower, when she got an image of Mary jumping off the bridge, the baby unwrapping from the swaddling and falling like a limp ragdoll to the rocks below. And the sound of the impact. She'd never forget that sound. She slid on her boxing gloves and started in on the heavy bag. Thunder looked at her, whined once, then went back to work on the tire, inching to the shade.

CHAPTER 23

"113 log and a unit to assist, respond to 102 W. Jefferson St., Franklin Towers, in refence to a DOA, possible suicide. Female down in the side access alley. 4th precinct is NUA. Respond code 1."

Goddamn, Park thought. Two jumpers in two days. And this one wasn't even in his precinct; NUA meaning no units available in 4th. They probably weren't out of roll call yet. He figured once he got there a 4th precinct unit would roll out and take the log. Until then...

"113 copies from 14th and Main St," Park transmitted.

"116 on the back," Shook answered up. "Coming from 25th and Cary."

"10-4, 113 and 116. Be advised paramedics on the scene and have pronounced," the dispatcher said, letting Park and Shook know that the victim had already been pronounced dead. On the way to the call, Park dialed Danny's number and put him on Bluetooth.

"You going over to Jefferson for the jumper?" Park asked when Danny answered.

"Who *is* this?" Danny asked.

"It's me. Park."

"No shit, Sherlock. I do have Caller ID you know. Such a doofas. Can't you even say, 'good morning' or 'hiya' or some ancient Asian greeting?"

Park hit the brakes so he wouldn't run over some guy crossing against the light with headphones on. "Why would I say, 'good morning' when it isn't?" Park asked, reasonably. "And stop with the Asian stuff. That's for my people only. No sharing."

"Whatever. I'm not going over there. I think Goldman might be taking it. His team is up today. I'm still tied up on the double from 30th street. They found the bodies up in Brooklyn. You up for a road trip if I have to go up there? Normally I'd take one of the Sidneys, but Kline's husband is almost done with his pilot's training and I don't know the other one all that good."

"Well," Park corrected.

"Well what?" Danny asked.

"You don't know her all that well. Not good."

Park hit a pothole and the SUV bounced once then settled.

"I thought your tribe was good at math, not grammar. Or is it 'well' at math?" Danny asked.

"113 is 10-23," Park transmitted. Then to Danny, "We're good at everything. Ok, I'm pulling up. Looks like a dead one in the alley."

"Goldman should be there in a minute or two. Hell, it's just across the street practically, so he may just walk. Before you hang up, how's Sharon? I heard you guys had a tough one on the bridge yesterday."

"116 is 10-23 as well," Shook came over the radio, pulling up right behind Park.

"She's taking it pretty hard, but she's got a tough hide. She'll learn to stow it away over time, deal with it. Just like we all do. Gotta go," Park said, ending the call.

CHAPTER 24

Danny put his cell back in his pocket and went to get in his car. The woman who'd left a message on his voicemail identified herself as Barbara Meyer. She didn't give Danny too much information over the phone but said that she knew Defreitis and wanted to pass some information on to Danny. She had suggested that Danny come to her house, but since he was riding solo now, he told her he'd rather meet at a coffeehouse. He'd said it was so he could have his morning fix, but it was actually to avoid any kind of accusations that could be levied against a male detective by a female informant.

He'd looked her up in RMS (the RPD database) and saw that she'd had a few drug arrests within the last few years, but no assaults. They'd agreed to meet in Henrico County, at one of the smaller coffee joints near the city line. While Danny did miss patrol work, he didn't miss being tied down to one geographical area, which was inherent in patrol work. As a detective, he had the freedom to go where his investigations took him.

He'd told her what kind of car he was driving, and he made sure he got to the coffee joint before she did. She pulled up a few minutes later, parked her car, and sat on one of the benches outside of the shop. She was a middle-aged woman, wearing glasses, a light summer shirt, and khaki pants. He walked up to her and introduced himself, then:

"You want to go inside and get some coffee, Barbara? My treat?"

"No thanks, Det. Jacobs. I just have a few minutes. I just want you to know that I'm clean, ok? I know you looked me up and saw my coke arrests. That's in my past, ok? Nine months sober."

"That's great, Barbara; congratulations."

But she moved on, ignoring his platitude. "Look, I feel bad for that lady who got killed. Troy? I couldn't give a fuck. That guy was a straight dealer. Didn't even try to hide it. You know he's married?" Danny shook his head no.

"Yep. Got a wife in Brooklyn, but he takes Bernadette with him whenever he makes drug runs. Pussy on the hoof. Poor thing. I guarantee you she just got killed because she was with him. Guaran-fucking-tee." Danny nodded to keep her talking.

"I used to buy my coke from Troy. For years. He'd always run from Brooklyn to Richmond. When he was first starting out, he'd make the runs on the China bus. Then when he started making some real money, he'd use rental cars. About six months ago, he brought in Defreitis. Like an apprentice. Showing him the ropes. But Defreitis had bigger plans and thought he was better than Troy. You could just tell by listening to him talk. Always said that he was 'coast-to-coast' or some shit. I bet he killed Troy to take his spot in the chain."

"You know he killed them as a fact, or that's just what you think?" Danny asked.

"Everyone up in Brooklyn knew they were dead before they got found. And everyone was saying that Defreitis is the one who killed them. Before you locked him up," she replied.

"How'd you know he was locked up?" Danny asked. "We never released that to the press."

"See what I'm saying? The street knows before anyone else. Of course, his dumbass has probably been calling people and telling them he got arrested, bragging about it. So that one's not a big mystery."

"Good point," admitted Danny.

"I have to get going," she said. "I've got a job interview at one of the nursing homes in the west end. I got my LPN degree through the recovery program. I just want to stay clean, you know?"

"Thanks, Barbara. And good luck. Do you mind if I reach out to you if anything else comes up? I won't call, just text."

"Texting's fine. See you later," she said, walking back to her car. Danny was all for supporting people battling their addictions and recovering from them. But he wasn't sure he'd want a recovering crackhead taking care of his grandfather in his golden years. Maybe it was just the cop in him.

CHAPTER 25

"I swear to God, officer, I had no idea this would happen," one of the roommates sobbed to Park. "We were all sitting around, just having a good time, then this."

'This' being the crumpled body of a 19yr old girl lying face down in a side alley. When she impacted, she suffered a compound fracture of the right leg, another compound fracture of her left arm, and one side of her skull was caved in. That was just what Park could see. He was sure most of her internal organs were destroyed from the fall. One of her eyes was open and staring at Park as he talked to the roommate. (Bodies aren't covered with sheets. If available, mobile barriers will be placed around a body to hide it from the public view while the police do their jobs processing the scene).

"Whose idea was it to take LSD?" Park asked.

"Tony's," she said. "He had a connect in Henrico, so he texted him, and then we all went out there to get it."

"Where in Henrico?" Park asked, writing in his pad as she was talking. Shook walked over from where he had been speaking with a construction worker who had seen the girl fall.

"It was some apartment complex off of Glenside, near 64," which would be Interstate 64; the highway that ran east-west through the city. "Tony texted him, then we all drove out there to get it. The dude came out of the house with one of those house arrest ankle monitors on. He gave Tony the foil packets, they dapped, and then we came back to Sara's apartment to do it."

Pam, the roommate, looked over at the body and began sobbing again. Park wasn't sympathetic to her tears; she was still alive to cry while Sara lay broken and bleeding on the concrete ground.

"And………?" Park asked.

Pam sniffed, then continued, "So, we all do our tab and everyone is getting real mellow. It's me, Sara, and Tony. Out of nowhere, Sara starts talking crazy. Say that she sees demons and devils. Says they're carrying bloody heads on swords."

Shook looked over at the body, then back to Pam.

"Then she starts complaining about how hot it was in the room and starts taking off her pants. Tony is like, 'I'm out,' and walks out of the room. I go to the door to call him back and I hear the window slide open. When I look, I see Sara climbing through and then she jumps! Just like that. Not a word. I ran over to the window and looked out. That's when I saw her down here." More sobs and sniffling.

"So, I scream and start running down the hallway to the stairwell. The elevator in this building is so fucking slow. As I'm running, I'm telling people to call 911. When I got outside, this is how I found her."

"How many times have all of you done LSD?" Park asked.

"Tony and I do it a lot. This was Sara's first time. She said that she wanted to try it."

"So, you let her try it on the 23rd floor of an apartment building with an unlocked window?" Shook asked. "Un-fucking believable. Can I talk to you over here a second, Park?" Park nodded, and they walked toward the body, away from Pam.

"So, the construction worker? He had come out of the building across the street there for a cigarette." Shook pointed at the building. "He was looking over at this building, when he sees our vic climb out of the window and just fall. He couldn't believe it. He didn't see anyone behind her when she went out. Though he did see afterward, I guess it was your girl, someone look out the window and then down at the ground. He said it sounded like a bag of concrete when she hit the ground."

"Yeah," Park said. "One of the workers in the building right next to the alley didn't see her fall but said that the ground shook when she hit."

"That guy Tony, still around?" Shook asked.

"No, he hasn't been seen since the vic started freaking out. I put out a BOLO on the air. Didn't you hear it?" Park answered.

Shook reached down and checked to see if his portable radio was on (after years on the street, it becomes second nature to reach down and check the knob on top of your portable to see if it's on, adjust the volume, etc.).

"Shit," Shook exclaimed. "It was off. Sorry."

Park grunted and looked over his notes, making sure that he got all the info he'd need for the report. Once the detectives arrived, they'd get most of the same information, but Park was a perfectionist and liked to make sure his reports were complete (many times, Major Crimes cases were solved because of complete reports and field interviews done by patrol officers).

"Officer?" Pam said.

"What?"

"There goes Tony right there," she said, pointing at a guy slinking around near the corner of the building; the same guy who took off running when he heard her say his name.

* * *

Anthony woke up feeling more refreshed than he had in months. He cranked the car up to get the defrost going, then looked around before unlocking his door and getting out; everything looked fine. He got out and stretched his back out, leaning left and right until it popped. He saw a homeless guy emerge from the woods behind the store and considered pulling out his rifle and shooting the guy in the chest. Then he wondered if he was losing his mind. Before the bank robbery, there's no way he would have had a thought to kill a stranger for no reason. But that was all BR, Before Robbery. Now he was AR, and he had the bloodlust. While he was having his internal monologue, the homeless guy's survival radar must have gone off and he scurried back into the woods. Missed opportunity, Anthony thought, then shrugged. Lots more opportunity in Richmond. He got back in his car and headed out to southbound I-95. Next stop? RVA.

CHAPTER 26

"So, can we charge him with dealing coke to my crackhead turned nurse?" Danny asked Peck, in reference to Defreitis.

"I thought it was straight cocaine, not crack," Peck countered.

"It was," said Danny. "But 'crackhead' sounds better."

Peck rolled her eyes as she looked over Danny's notes and compared them with Defreitis' record. "He's been charged with a ton of drug related stuff, but zero convictions. That's the kind of thing that drives me crazy. Everything either dismissed, not prosecuted, or he gets found guilty of a lesser misdemeanor charge."

Danny checked his phone while she was going through the record. He saw that he'd gotten an email from the Sidneys. Since it was initially a missing person case, then a double homicide, the lab was able to put a rush on the comparisons between the victim's blood and the blood found on Defreitis' pants. He clicked on the email to download the PDF and Bingo!! It was a match.

"Hey, Peck? Check this out." But Peck was still looking at the criminal record and talking to herself.

"Peck!!"

"What, Danny, damn!? I'm trying to sort through this."

"Just got the lab back. The blood on the pants matches the victims' blood!"

"How'd you get the victim's DNA when they were found in New York?" Peck asked.

"The New York Medical Examiner's Office sent the sample next-day down to our lab. Then they rushed the results. Bam!"

"That's great, Danny, but it's just another piece in the puzzle. Remember how he told you that he hugged both of them when he saw them here? And how he drove that rental car?" Peck asked.

"Sure. So, he could explain away any of *his* DNA that may be on them or in the car."

"Exactly," said Peck. "And to explain away the victim's blood on his pants, he'll say that he went into the house looking for them and must have gotten some of their blood on his pants when he was looking. That's if he even talks to you the second time you take a run at him. He may just lawyer up right away."

Danny was getting pissed, but then realized what she said about interviewing him a second time. "So, by saying a 'second time' does that mean you'll ok me getting warrants for selling to the crackhead?"

Peck threw the record on her desk and said, "Sure. Just know that we won't be able to go forward if your CI (confidential informant) won't testify. But it'll be a new charge against Defreitis and that gives you a second chance to talk to him."

Standing up and putting his phone back in his pocket, Danny stated, "Works for me."

CHAPTER 27

"I thought you said that Thunder doesn't speak English," Officer Martin "Marty" Edwards said to Sharon.

"I don't know of any dog who speaks English. Or horse, or cat. If you're hearing animals speak English, Marty, you may need to go talk to the city shrink," Sharon suggested.

They were standing on the top deck of the old HQ building, which was right across the street from the John Marshall Courthouse. Marty had just finished up with traffic court and had sent Sharon a message on her MDT to meet him. Old HQ was the most convenient spot since she and Thunder were rolling around downtown today. Marty worked in 1st Precinct on Church Hill and the old HQ building was on the way back to the precinct. The old police building was scheduled for destruction to make room for another glass tower, courtesy of the university. It was good riddance, though, since the old HQ was built back when asbestos was the way to go.

"You're such a dick, Sharon," Marty retorted. Thunder growled a little at the insult, then snapped the air once, letting Marty know he'd heard that.

"See? He knows what I said," Marty complained. Then to Thunder, "And you." Thunder turned his head to the side, giving him the eye. "Don't give me any shit. If it weren't for me, your bones would be dissolving in the belly of a pit bull."

Thunder farted, then licked his balls, very slowly. "Gross," said Marty.

"He was *trained* to follow commands that were given to him in Czech," she explained. "But he picks up English words on his own. How could he not? What's the best way to learn a language?"

Marty was getting ready to answer but Sharon cut him off. "Rhetorical question. The best way is to live in the country and immerse yourself in the language. That's what Thunder does every day, dealing with cops and drones alike. He's bilingual." Which got another bark out of Thunder and a smile to go along with it.

Before Marty could continue with the debate, the radio squawked:

"116, foot pursuit!!" Shook yelled.

* * *

Park jumped in his SUV as Shook took off chasing Tony over to Broad St. He hit the lights and sirens, but didn't get on the air, choosing to let Shook call in the foot pursuit since he was right behind him.

"116, he's running eastbound on Broad from Second Street. Wearing long, camo pants, black t-shirt, white sneakers."

"Radio copies, 116. You have the air. Units respond code 1."

Tony was running past the new boutiques and art galleries on Broad, running into passerby on the sidewalk, pushing them out of his way. Shook was about a half block behind him, running full on, one hand on his shoulder mic, calling it in as he went. Tony looked over his shoulder to see where Shook was and accidentally veered off the sidewalk, into the street. He corrected his path just as a city bus was driving by, nearly making him a puddle in the street.

Park made a screeching turn onto Broad from Second Street and saw the bus almost end the foot pursuit. Traffic was heavy, and he got stuck behind other cars that were slowing to see what was going on. One car stopped completely, causing another one to rear end it with a crash. Park was able to stop in time to avoid another accident, but cars had also stopped in the center lane, right by his SUV, effectively trapping Park in his car.

Shook heard the crash to his rear, but his adrenaline was flowing, and he was gaining on Tony. "116 to radio, coming up on Fourth and Broad!" Shook transmitted. He could hear sirens coming to him, but he'd have this one all wrapped up before you knew it, he thought. Which was when Tony stopped running, grabbed a woman by her collar, put her in a headlock, then put a gun to her head.

Shook skid to a stop, feet away from Tony and his hostage. He pulled his gun and said, "Let her go, motherfucker!! Do it now!!" He was trying to line up his gun sights right on Tony's forehead, but he kept ducking behind the woman. Her eyes were wide and terrified, her hand clawing at the arm around her throat. Shook wasn't even sure if she knew there was a gun pressed against her head, she was so focused on the arm. "Let her the fuck GO!!" Shook commanded.

Park was trapped in his car; he couldn't squirm over to the passenger side because of all the center console MDT equipment. And it was a total logjam of cars on the driver's side with everyone stopped to watch the drama. Park got on the radio:

"113 to radio! 116's got one at gunpoint. Suspect has a hostage. They're at the corner of Fourth and Broad, on Broad. Suspect is armed and has the gun to the hostage's head. Units proceed with caution and watch for crossfire." *FUCK!!* Park *had* to get out and help Shook.

There was no talking to this guy, Shook thought. His eyes were crazy and not focused. He was gripping the woman tighter and tighter with his left arm, moving the gun from her head to her neck with the right hand. She was tugging frantically at the arm around her neck, screaming at Shook to help her. Every time Tony's head would show itself, Shook's gun tracked it, but then Tony would move his head back behind his hostage. A movie line popped into Shook's head: *Sometimes you have to shoot the hostage.* Shook's finger tightened on the trigger.

Tony screamed like he'd been shot when Thunder came up from behind and bit down into his upper thigh and ass, ripping and tearing like he was playing with his old tire in the backyard. Thunder had hit him so hard, Tony had let go of the gun and the hostage at the same time. The hostage scrambled behind Shook as he stepped forward with his foot and scooted the gun away from Tony. Tony had other things on his mind or more accurately, one thing on his ass: Thunder. "Get it off me!! Get it off me!! I'm sorry!!! Please, get it off me!!" Thunder had dragged Tony to the ground and was just holding on to him.

Sharon told him to release and Marty came over and cuffed Tony's hands behind his back, Tony whimpering the whole time. Shook covered him as Marty pulled some gloves from his belt and searched Tony for any additional weapons. He pulled a few silver tabs out of Tony's right pants pocket and showed them to Shook. "Probably the rest of the LSD,"

Shook said. Marty handed it to Shook as he finished the search.

"He's good to go," Marty said, rolling him over on to his chewed-up ass. "OUCCCCCHHHH!!!!" cried Tony. "Tough shit, dickhead," Marty whispered to him, but letting him lie on his side.

"That was awesome timing, you guys," Shook said. Sharon held up a finger and told radio that the suspect was in custody and the hostage wasn't injured; though they would need the medics for Tony. When she was done, "No problem. We aim to please. Now, someone needs to get Park the rest of the way out of his car."

They all looked over and saw that Park had rolled his driver's window down and was attempting to climb out of it. Unluckily, it was a tight squeeze and Park was stuck, not unlike Winnie the Pooh stuck in a tree. "Hey, Park!" Sharon shouted. "Get your honey?", not being able to resist the Pooh Bear reference.

CHAPTER 28

"What do you mean he got a bond? We like him for a double murder!" Danny was on the phone with the clerk over at the courthouse. "No," Danny continued, "We haven't actually charged him yet." He was silent as the clerk explained that the judge had looked at his record, seen nothing violent and granted him a bond. "But what about the fleeing from the police when they tried to stop him?"

"Misdemeanor eluding. No injuries," replied the clerk.

"I was just heading over to the Magistrates Office to get a felony warrant for distribution," Danny said.

"What can I tell you, detective? You should have gotten over there earlier. He's out."

"Shit. How big was his bond?"

"Standard for traffic offenses. Low. PR bond." Meaning he got out on his own personal recognizance and would only have to pay if he didn't show up for court. Which, Danny knew, he wouldn't.

Danny hung up with the clerk, then called Peck. "Yeah, yeah. I heard," Peck said when she answered the phone. "No big surprise. Look on the bright side; you get the drug warrants for him, Cindy catches him again, and maybe he's dirty. Transporting drugs or with a gun."

"Yeah, I guess," Danny said with a sigh.

"Look, it may be a blessing in disguise," Peck continued. "You and I both know he did the double, but we've got no witnesses, no murder weapon, and no confession. He gave that bullshit excuse for the possibility of DNA transfer, but with the right jury, they'd acquit. And if more evidence popped up after the acquittal, we'd be fucked since we can't try him twice."

Danny understood. Going to trial when there was a possibility of more evidence being found later was a gamble. If you put on a circumstantial case and won, fantastic. If you put it on and lost, then you later find either a witness or a key piece of evidence, it can never be used because of double jeopardy rules. Because of this, many cases stayed open indefinitely, frustrating the victim's families and detectives.

"Ok, Peck. I'll let you know when the warrants are on file and I send Cindy out hunting." Peck was fine with that and hung up. Danny's double was on pause.

CHAPTER 29

Once Park had gotten himself unstuck from the car window, with the help of Shook and the traffic getting moving again, they headed down to the hospital to keep an eye on Tony while he was treated for the dog bite to his ass. All prisoners who had either received injuries prior to their arrest or a direct result of their arrest had to get medically cleared at the university hospital. This could be a lengthy process and was boring as hell. In fact, recently a midnight shift officer had fallen asleep while waiting for a prisoner to be treated for some chest pain. The prisoner was uncuffed to allow for a thorough test and simply walked out of the exam room when the officer had nodded off.

Park and Shook were standing in the room with the ER doc while he put a stitch or two in Tony's ass. "Man, that HURTS!" Tony cried as the doc worked. "Stop squirming around or I may sew up the wrong hole," replied the doctor.

Park pulled out his phone to see what time it was and saw a missed call from Abad; service in the ER was wonky at best. "Hey, Shook? You got him? I need to make a call." Shook nodded and kept on watching the doc work. Park stepped outside to the ambulance entrance and called Abad's number.

"Abad? It's Park. Saw you called, what's up?" Abad started talking just as an ambulance rolled down the lane, code one. The driver had turned off the siren just before entering, but the echo of it bounced around in the enclosed driveway completely drowning out Abad's voice. "HOLD ON!" Park yelled. "I NEED TO MOVE INTO THE COURTYARD!" Park walked the fifty feet out of the drive and into the patient courtyard.

"Ok. I'm back," Park said.

"I'm going to get right to it, Park; I'm quitting," Abad said. "I've got a feeling that they're going to drag this thing out, eventually make me a civilian and put me down in Property permanently. There's no way in hell I can do this for 27 more years until I retire." He was referring to the fact that non-sworn employees can't retire with a pension until they do 30 years; sworn employees can leave at 25 years with a full pension. Abad had 3 years in, so he'd have to pull 27 more to get his 30.

"Damn, Abad. That's fucked up. You sure you don't want to hang in and see what happens?" Park asked.

"No way. You think I want to be a civilian down there, watching tons of cops come in day after day, talking about what they've been doing on the street? Bringing in guns and drugs, talking about how they got them? All the guys looking at me, knowing I used to be one of them. No way. Not for me."

Park knew that he couldn't do that either. Just like Abad said; no way. "So, what're you going to do?" Park asked.

"I've still got my law enforcement certifications," Abad said. "I think I may go up north and try to get on one of the Jersey departments just outside of New York. Maybe Jersey City, Linden, or Weehawken. Hopefully one of them will take me on."

"I'm sure they will," said Park. "You're a fantastic cop, Abad. We're gonna miss you."

"Thanks, Park. I'll miss you guys, too. And who knows? Maybe I'll come across the bank robber that got away up there. I hear he's from New York. Anyway, I gave my two weeks, but today's it for me. The supervisor down in Property is cool and said I can burn a few days in sick leave and comp. Keep my number Park. And stay in touch, ok?"

"Will do, Abad. Take care." Park took a deep breath and considered walking back into the hospital but changed his mind and took a seat in the courtyard. Shook would text him or call him on the radio when Tony was ready to go. Park never realized the patient courtyard was so nice; shaded benches, burbling fountain in the center. All very relaxing. Made sense he guessed. Patients needed some respite from the interior of the hospital, and this was a pleasant space for them. Truth was, Park needed some respite himself.

He'd heard of stories like Abad's before; good cops caught up in bad situations where the cop feels forced to resign because of political posturing by city officials. Especially in the anti-cop climate of the present. Park considered himself lucky that he hadn't gotten caught up in anything like that. Yet, that is. He'd been doing patrol work for over 20 years. Was he overdue for a viral video outrage over some arrest he makes where he has to use force? Why hadn't it happened to him yet? Poor Abad had only been on the street for a few years and was thrust into that combat situation, only to be judged by an asshole IA investigator with not much more time on the street than Abad. If Park got put in the same situation, would he stick it out and trust the city to back him up, or would he pull the plug and take a retirement?

Just as Park was slipping toward melancholy over the state of policing, he saw a young motor officer from Henrico County leaving the Ambulance Entrance on his BMW. The motor guy looked left and right for traffic, then saw Park sitting on the bench. He gave Park the 'hang loose' hand signal, nodded his head, and roared off. Park, an avid motorcycle rider himself, had recently finished a ride from DC to New York, escorted by motor cops from multiple jurisdictions the entire 200 some odd miles. They blocked off the highways, then the side streets in all the small townships of New Jersey, then into Manhattan. Park remembered the feeling of pride and brotherhood as the motor officers leapfrogged past the riders the entire route, confident that they could protect the riders, no matter where the cops were from or what town or city, they were in.

Park's phone buzzed with an incoming text from Shook:

You taking a shit or something? This asshole's done, and I want to get out of here. Let's go!

Faith restored, Park sent an emoji of a middle finger and a turd, then went in to go take the asshole to jail.

CHAPTER 30

"How do you and Thunder always seem to be in the right place at the right time?" Marty asked. They were back at the kennels, where Sharon preferred doing her paperwork. If she went to one of the precincts, she'd have to leave Thunder in the back of the SUV while she typed away inside. Police dogs weren't pets and couldn't just hang out inside the precincts with the officers. Some of them were truly nuts and just liked biting people. Think it's not true? Ask a K9 officer.

Thunder wasn't nuts, but he also was not a fan of anyone other than a select few petting him. Marty had recently made the list for helping Thunder out of a sticky situation last summer involving a pit bull and Thunder's leg, but it was a guest spot and subject to revocation at Thunder's discretion. Thunder was currently sitting on the floor, chewing a piece of car tire that Sharon kept in her desk drawer.

"Hey, you were there, too. Remember? Plus, you were there when Thunder was getting eaten by that pit," she said. Thunder took offense at that and turned his back to her and kept on chewing.

"Now you pissed him off," Marty said. Thunder's left ear raised, listening.

"He'll be ok. The big baby," Sharon said. Thunder lowered his ear and thumped his tail once but kept his back to them.

"I swear that dog knows what we're saying," Marty said. "Like communicating with one of those apes that know sign language." Thunder's hair bristled, and he let loose a low growl at being compared to an ape.

"There," Sharon said as she finished typing and stretched her back until it popped. "Now what were you saying?"

"I can't remember," said Marty. "Anyway, how're you doing after that lady and her baby on the bridge? That was some terrible shit."

"I'm ok, I guess. It helped to find out that the baby was already dead. Park and I talked about it; both of us at the time couldn't have cared less for her. We were pissed that she brought that baby out there with her. We judged her unfairly, Marty. That baby was the only good thing to come from what happened to her and she died. Did you hear the medical examiner thought the baby probably died from SIDS or co-sleeping?" This last sentence said with a hitch in her voice. Thunder heard and came over to sit beside her.

Marty shook his head no and stayed silent.

"The only good thing," she repeated, "and she may have accidentally killed her child. And we were mad at her. That poor woman." Sharon began sobbing and lowered her head to Thunder's neck. Marty was wary about approaching her, so he let himself out while she grieved.

CHAPTER 31

"That railing is crooked," Park commented.

"Bullshit if it is," retorted Danny. "I used a level and everything, just because I knew you'd say that shit. Your ass is crooked."

"I'm telling you, it's crooked. I can tell just by eyeballing it," Park replied. Danny opened his mouth to say something, but Park beat him to it. "And don't go saying anything about how my Asian eyes can't see straight."

Danny closed his mouth without saying anything and threw Park a level. "I'll bet you 5 dollars it's level," Danny said.

"Wow. 5 whole dollars? You must be certain," said Park. "You're on." He walked over to the railing, held his thumb out in front of it and looked at it with one eye closed. "Can you see anything at all like that?" Danny asked. "Shut it, round-eye," Park responded, as he placed the level on the railing.......

* * *

"I can't believe you're sitting here on my deck, drinking my sodas after taking 5 dollars from me," Danny complained.

"Believe it," Park chided.

"Moving forward," said Danny, "I heard about Abad. That's some fucking bullshit. But I don't blame him for leaving. Since Webb already left, I can see Abad getting used as a scapegoat."

"Neither one of them should be used as a scapegoat. No cop ever should," Park said.

"I agree. Abad's a great cop. He'll land another gig up north. Here's to him." They clinked drinks and settled back into their chairs. It was taking a long, long time for the two men to finish redoing Danny's deck. They'd work for an hour or two, get to talking and arguing, then settle in for drinks in the chairs. Though neither would admit it, both had no desire for the job to get done.

Danny didn't want to bring up the situation on the bridge again. He'd heard that the baby was already dead from probable co-sleeping, and he knew how the baby came to be conceived. He also knew that Park was feeling awful about being mad at Mary but recognized that Park would have to work through that on his own. He did want to know how Sharon was doing; he knew Park worried about his daughter.

"How's Sharon?" he asked.

"She's dealing with it the best she can," Park responded. "She broke down with me on the bridge right after; and before I came over here, she said she had another minor melt down while she and that guy Marty were at the kennels."

"Marty, the guy who killed that pit bull?" Danny asked.

"That's the one. He's a good kid. Saved Thunder's ass for sure. It would have killed Sharon if Thunder got killed right in front of her. She'd probably never recover from that."

They were quiet for a few minutes, then Danny changed the subject.

"I talked to Amos Simms about that LSD case," Danny said. Amos was also a Major Crimes detective. "He talked to that female junkie some more and found out that the dealer is under some kind of house arrest with the Sheriff's Office. Like a work release program."

"Ok," Park said, fishing around in the cooler for another drink. It was hit or miss with Danny's drink selections; half the time they were some weird shit from the bottom shelf of deep discount stores.

"So, since he's technically an inmate, the sheriff deputies got a search warrant because of the LSD angle and went to his house," Danny continued.

"Uh-huh," Park said, pulling a bottle out of the cooler and holding it up to look at the label; yep, never heard of it. He plopped it back in the cooler and dug back in for a water, the safest bet from the discount stores.

"They go in the house and take him into custody and sit his ass in one of their cars. They find a cell phone in his room, and his mom, who he's living with since he got out of jail, tells them that she pays the bill on the phone, so it's hers. She gives them the passcode and they search the text messages."

Park cracked open the water, took a sip and then spit it out. "What the hell??!!"

"You don't like it? That's pickle water. It was on sale. It's great for replacing electrolytes," Danny explained.

Park threw it in the trash and said, "I owe you a dime for that," and added, "I want change."

"So anyway," Danny continued, "The guy texts Tony, 'I got the best LSD around!' Wham, bam, and goddamn. A slam dunk case for contributing to that girl's death."

"What an idiot," Park said. "Well, I got to get up early in the morning," he said, stretching out his back. "I'll see you around. And thanks for asking about Sharon. I appreciate it."

Danny nodded and bumped fists with his best friend.

* * *

Anthony had gotten a little behind in his schedule. He'd wanted to get to Richmond early in the day, but when he got back on the highway from Fredericksburg, he'd been thinking about how the blood squirted up from the driver's head and had gotten on I-95 northbound instead of southbound! He hadn't noticed until he was well into DC, then he got stuck in traffic. Again. By the time he'd gotten off of the highway, gotten some gas with the absolute last of his money and gotten back on southbound, he was beyond pissed. This time traffic was backed up south of Fredericksburg. When he finally got through it, he couldn't stand driving slow anymore, so he accelerated up to 85mph, just to blow off steam. That's when he saw the Virginia State Trooper car hit its blue lights behind him.

CHAPTER 32

"What the hell is wrong with me?" Sharon asked Thunder. They were working an evening shift tonight, 1500hrs-0230hrs. Two of the things Sharon loved about being in K9 were being able to work different shifts and to go all over the city. Many times, she'd get called out to the surrounding counties if they didn't have a K9 team working or theirs was tied up. She got all the freedom of a detective, but still got to do patrol work. Plus, she got to be with Thunder; the best thing of all.

Thunder was currently chewing on a piece of tire he'd snatched from the kennel. When she asked the question, he looked up from the chew, then got back to it, assuming it was rhetorical.

"I mean, I *never* breakdown. You know this. But now I've done it twice. I mean, what the fuck??" Thunder didn't have any answers for her, but he didn't mind listening. "I need to get my shit straight," she said. "I can't be breaking down in front of the guys."

"Radio to K-5?" breaking into her conversation.

"K-5, go ahead," she answered.

"Can you assist state police with a pursuit coming into the city from 95?"

"10-4, radio. Where are they coming from? Any idea what exit?" Sharon asked.

"They're inbound from 95, heading south. Closest exit would be the Chamberlayne Ave. exit."

"10-4. Switch me over to the pursuit channel," she directed. The pursuit channel was a centralized channel that the dispatchers could switch pursuing officers to in order to free up the regular channels for normal traffic.

Sharon hit the lights and sirens on her SUV and started rolling to the northern end of the city. "Ready to get the bad guys, boy?" she asked. Thunder barked with glee. Always!!!

CHAPTER 33

Danny was scheduled to work an evening shift as well. Unlike the patrol schedule which was for permanent days or midnights (12-hour shifts), the Major Crimes detectives' schedules changed every week. There was a pattern, but it was a complicated one, where one week you'd work one evening shift, then the next you'd work two. It was always a combination of evening shifts and day shifts.

When he got in at 1500hrs, he saw the red light on his phone lit up. Message. He punched in his password and, "Hey Det. Jacobs? Major Ames over at the Justice Center. We've got a guy over here, name of.........Reggie Taylor? He says he knows you. Anyway, he said that he's got some information on one of your cases. I'm not sure what time you come in, but you can come over here whenever you want to talk to him. Ok, bye."

Reggie? Danny thought. *What does that asshole want?* Danny thought. The last time he and Park had tried to talk to him, he'd basically told them to fuck off. He'd gotten a few years in prison for all the shit he'd put them through last year but was apparently still at the Justice Center until they could find a prison that had room for him.

Danny checked his calendar and saw that he was free for the next couple of hours, so he may as well go see what he wanted. He shot Park a text:

Hey. Guess who wants to talk to me at the jail?

Danny saw that Park was typing, then:

I'm busy. Who?

Grouch, Danny thought. He typed:

Motherfucking Reggie, that's who.

Danny waited again, then got Park's reply:

Give him this for me (followed by the middle finger emoji).

Danny pulled up at the Justice Center, traded his police ID for a Visitor ID, put all of his weapons in a gun box, then waited in the Contact Visitation room. After a few minutes, Reggie shuffled in, wearing an orange jail suit that looked a few sizes too big for him. He'd been shot before he could leave town last summer, and by the looks of him, he hadn't been able to eat too much since the shooting. His skin was pasty, and his hair was stringy, but you couldn't blame that on the jail; he always looked like that.

Reggie pulled the door shut behind him and Danny told him to sit down. Neither offered a hand to shake; Reggie because he was an asshole and Danny because he didn't want to get a staph infection.

"What do you want Reggie? You called me down here, so don't waste my time."

"Why do you have to act like such a dick, dude. Damn," Reggie said.

Ignoring him, Danny said, "I'm waiting."

"Ok, man. Look, I want to get some time knocked off of my sentence. This food in here tastes like shit. I can't keep anything down. The shooting messed up my insides anyway. I need some good stuff to eat. I'm turning to dust here."

"No promises, Reggie. You know that. I'll write down what you tell me and take it to the prosecutor. If it's any good, it might help you out and I'll put a word in for you."

"Not good enough. I want a guarantee," Reggie said.

"Bye, dick face," Danny said, standing to leave.

"Wait, wait. Hold up. C'mon man."

"Tell me what you've got. I'll tell the prosecutor. Take it or leave it," Danny said.

"Ok. Sit down, man. Damn."

"I'll stand."

"Look, man. I was in the cell with that guy from New York. That Defreitis guy? He told me he killed that couple, man."

Danny sat down.

Anthony was the target of a full-blown pursuit now. He had no idea where the other two cop cars came from, but they joined in with the first guy within minutes. Anthony planned to take out as many of them as he could with the rifle, but decided he'd have a better chance of doing more damage on one of the side streets. He saw an exit coming up fast and took it, steadying the rifle with his right hand as he drove with the left. He was glad Duane had made him get used to shooting one-handed; it would come in handy today.

CHAPTER 34

"Bark, Bark, Bark!! K5, we're in the pursuit! *Bark, bark, bark!!"* Sharon transmitted; Thunder adding background ambiance.

"10-4, K5. State police is calling it."

Thunder was excited and still barking, so Sharon decided against transmitting again. The pursuit had come in from I-95 like radio had predicted and was currently going southbound on Chamberlayne Ave. Leaving her SUV's radio on the pursuit channel, she clicked on her portable unit and used her shoulder mic to transmit with one hand, while driving with the other.

"Bark, Bark....K5 on 4....bark, bark, BARK!!"

"Go ahead K5. Try to quiet down your partner," Radio responded.

"BARK!!........Thunder, Klid!!......Klid!!....," Sharon told Thunder in Czech. While he did understand English words, when they were working, she used Czech to let him know it was work and not play.

"K5, I'm about 3 cars back. We're southbound on Chamberlayne Avenue, passing Azalea. State's on the pursuit channel. I'll transmit on 4 to let the guys know where we are...approaching Westbrook."

The State Police guys were advising the dispatcher on the pursuit channel the same thing as far as direction of travel. Sharon put both hands back on the wheel and focused on driving. In front of her were three Virginia State Police cars, two marked and one unmarked. She saw that one of the marked units had 'K9' on the rear quarter panel. She wondered which Trooper it was.

Anthony kept the car under control with his left hand and braced the rifle on the back of the front passenger seat with his right. He looked over his right shoulder, down the length of the barrel, then fired off five shots through his rear windshield.

The car they were after was a medium sized four-door sedan. She couldn't see the license plate. All five cars turned onto Westbrook Avenue, heading toward Brook Road. She'd straightened her wheels and was accelerating when she saw flashes of light coming from the suspect car, followed by unmistakable sounds of assault rifle fire, and then the light bar atop the lead Trooper car exploding.

The lead car peeled off to the side of the road, striking the curb and bouncing up onto the grass. The sedan barreled through the intersection, running the red light, the second Trooper right behind him. The second Trooper car, the unmarked, almost made it through but got hit in the left quarter panel by a box truck that had the green light on Brook Road. The Trooper's car spun around and wound up on the concrete median, facing the wrong way for that lane of traffic.

That left the K9 Trooper and Sharon. Both slowed down to clear the intersection, then punched it, accelerating again. When she cleared the intersection, she saw RPD units rolling down Brook, lights and sirens going, coming to join the pursuit. It would be over by the time they got to her.

* * *

Anthony saw the first Trooper car jerk over to the side of the road as a result of his gunshots. He turned back around to steer and just barely missed getting turned into a hood ornament by a box truck going down the road. He saw the truck take out the second Trooper car in his rear-view mirror. Still two cops back there. He brought the gun back up on the seat, took one more look out the front windshield, then turned around and aimed out the back again.

* * *

"K5 to radio!! We're taking gunfire! Sounds like an AR...!" Before she could finish her sentence, more flashes of light from the sedan. "Thunder! Dolu!! Down!!" telling him to get down on the floor of the SUV.

The sedan had taken a right turn into the abandoned Azalea Mall parking lot, rifle fire still coming from the car. The Trooper's car fishtailed, then straightened but not before a line of rifle rounds stitched the car lengthwise from rear to front, shredding both tires on the right side, disabling the car. Now Sharon and Thunder were the lead car and closing in fast.

CHAPTER 35

"Why would this guy tell you anything?" Danny asked, suspicious. "Just out of the blue, he tells you he murdered two people?"

"I swear he did, man. I don't know why. Maybe because he's not from here and it was weighing on him. You know, he had to get it off his chest."

Danny doubted that. From what he'd learned about Defreitis, he didn't have anything resembling a conscious. But Reggie heard about it somehow. "So, tell me what he said."

"Ok. He said that he knows the guy from up in New York; Brooklyn, I think. He knew of the girl, but not well. Like, he knew the guy was married, but this bitch wasn't his wife."

"Stop," Danny said, holding up his hand. "That's the first and last time you refer to the dead lady that way. Got it?"

"Damn, ok man. I didn't mean nothing by it. Shit."

Danny waited out his little tantrum, ignoring him and looking at his phone.

"So," Reggie continued, "The guy had brought him up in the drug game. They're all originally from Portugal or someplace. I can't remember where. But they stick together. Well, they at least deal drugs together. He said some of them may even be cops....."

"Stop," Danny said again. "Don't fucking even think about disparaging cops, understand? You think I want to hear what some scumbag, asshole, drug dealing murderer assumes about who's a cop?"

"Fine. Whatever," said Reggie. "So Defreitis, he says that he's like under this dude in the drug game, right? But Defreitis is cocky, he thinks he can do better. Sell more. Thinks this guy is all used up. So, he thinks up this plan."

When Danny was looking at his phone, he'd turned on the recorder, so he could listen to this later with Peck.

"He knows this guy is coming down here for one of the runs. He figures that he'd be better off doing the hit here in Richmond than up in New York. Too many people know him up there. So, he rents a car and drives down here, calling this guy when he gets to town. He goes to the address and the guy lets him in. Just another deal, right? Nope. Dude opens the door and Defreitis shoots him square in the chest. Guy falls out on the carpet, dead."

Reggie starts coughing and Danny pushes back to avoid whatever foul disease is trying to escape from Reggie's body.

"Sorry. Got prison cough. You know, like how dogs get kennel cough? Where was I? Oh yeah, so he shoots dude in the chest and kills him. But then he sees the bit...um...woman in the easy chair. She looks him right in the face. She's a witness, right? Bang, bang. Two in the grape. Now he's got two dead bodies. He puts one on top of the other and pulls up some carpet. Then he gets their rental car and backs it up to the rear door, through the alley. He shoves both of them in the trunk, then goes back inside to clean up."

"No one comes outside to see what's going on? No one heard the shot?" Danny asked.

"Up on the Hill? No way. You know how many times you hear gunshots up there? Lots. I bet cops only get called half the time when shots go off," Reggie said. "So, he's going around the place, trying to get all the blood up. He found some bleach under a sink, but there's not too much in the bottle. So, he's like fuck it. He said that he's turned his phone off when he got to the house, because he didn't want it ringing while he was taking care of business."

Danny made a note of this. He could check Defreitis' phone records and see when there was little to no activity. He'd learned that dealers *always* kept their phones on; it was how they did business.

"So, he leaves the house and drives up to New York in their rental car. Now *that* shit takes some balls. Driving a car with two bodies in the trunk 300 miles? He parks that bitch like a block or two from dude's house. He wanted it to look like someone from the neighborhood was leaving a message. You know, mob shit."

Reggie coughs some more, clears his throat, and spits on the floor at his feet; like he was outside.

"Defreitis thought he was home free, until you sicced Cindy on him. He knew that stolen car charge was bullshit. When you came to talk to him, he knew what you were after. That's why he didn't say shit. So that's it, man. What do you think?"

Danny sat back and considered. Reggie actually had some decent information that lined up with what Danny knew. Most of what Reggie said hadn't been released to the media, so he was looking more and more legit. He'd have to reach out to the New York M.E.'s office and confirm where the victims had been shot.

Reggie misinterpreted Danny's silence as disbelief and said, "Look, detective. I swear I'm telling you the truth. And I can tell you one more thing, so you *know* I'm telling the truth."

"Oh yeah," said Danny. "What?"

"I know where the gun is."

CHAPTER 36

The sedan had gone left once it entered the parking lot, heading toward a garden center that used to be a little 'Safety Town' with a small road and buildings, stop signs, and a stoplight on a stand. Usually a cop would be in there showing kids how they were supposed to cross the street safely, what the regulatory signs and signals meant. It was before Sharon's time, but Park had told her about it. She couldn't see a license plate on the rear of the car but noticed that the rear windshield had been peppered with bullet holes; whoever was shooting must have been firing out the back windshield.

Anthony slowed as he entered the parking lot; he raised his left knee up and steered with it as he dropped the magazine from the rifle and loaded his spare. Duane had trained him to always keep a spare magazine ready to go. He checked the mag he'd taken out and saw that it still had a few more rounds in it. Good. That meant he didn't need to charge the rifle to load the fresh round; it was still in battery and one was in the chamber. He put his knee back

down and took the wheel with his left hand, turning the car before he hit the dead end.

Now the sedan was heading toward the garden center getting closer to the dead end on that side of the lot. Sharon slowed down so as not to get too close to the car when it would inevitably stop. The driver figured it out quickly, however, and turned the wheel hard to the right, making the tires smoke. Sharon caught a glimpse at the front license plate as it made the turn: New York.

Anthony had the car pointing away from the dead end and saw that one of the cop cars was just behind him parallel to him. He sped up, pointed the rifle out the passenger window, then hit the brakes, lining up his shot.

She thought briefly that maybe this was the guy from the Fidelity Bank robbery a few months ago; New York ties plus an assault rifle. Her focus changed quickly as she saw the driver raise a rifle up, one handed, as he was driving and point it at her SUV. She jerked her steering wheel to the right, as the gun opened up. She could hear the rounds pinging and zipping off the side of her car then she heard Thunder squeal and yelp. She got in behind the sedan and pulled her gun out of its holster, then braced it on her dashboard, holding on to the wheel with her left hand. Using the SUV's hood as gun sights, she shot through her front windshield, seeing holes punch into the back of the sedan's trunk. *How do you like being the hunted now, motherfucker*, she thought.

"Holy fuck!!" Anthony cursed, *as the cop's rounds hit the back of his car.* This motherfucker is crazy, *he thought, raising his rifle again.*

The sedan swerved to the left, then right, and slowed suddenly bringing Sharon's SUV nearly abreast of it. She caught a quick glimpse of the rifle raising again. Steering wheel in her left hand, she reached across her body with her right hand and emptied her magazine into the driver's compartment of the car. She saw red splash on the car's windshield, then the car rolled slowly forward. Still steering with her left hand, she hit the mag release button on the pistol grip, the used mag falling into her lap. She lifted her left knee to the wheel and steered with it while grabbing a fresh magazine from her belt and jamming it into the pistol.

The sedan slowly veered to the left, striking a ramshackle wooden fence that had been erected around the old mall that used to be in this lot. Sharon got out of the SUV, seeing at least two RPD officers on her left. "Police!! Show me your hands!!" Sharon shouted. No answer. "Police!! Show me your hands right fucking NOW!!" she commanded. Still nothing. One of the other officers kept his gun aimed at the driver's side and approached the car. Sharon sidestepped to her right to also cover the driver's compartment while avoiding a crossfire with the officer on the other side.

The officer on the driver's side did a quick look into the car, then a longer look. "Clear," he said and holstered his gun. He looked over at Sharon, shook his head, making a cutting motion across his throat. "You got him. 10-7." Which was police talk for out of service, or in this case, dead. "You sure?" Sharon said, gun still out, but pointed to the ground. "Oh yeah. I'm pretty sure you need the top of your head to live. This guy is missing his. Looks like a bowl of porridge where his forehead was. I'm going to call the supervisor. You good?"

"Yeah, I'm good." She turned and saw another RPD officer was standing by the rear of her SUV, Thunder's area. Something wasn't right; Thunder should be barking his head off. Then she saw the bullet holes in the side of the SUV and ran over to the vehicle. "Get the fuck out of my way!!" she yelled at the startled officer. She opened the door and saw

Thunder lying motionless on the floor of the SUV, back to her. "Oh no......," she wailed.

CHAPTER 37

"Fuck, I hate dealing with inmates," Peck complained. Danny had gone by her office after leaving the jail. He had been inside with Reggie for over an hour and missed the state police pursuit, and Peck had gotten tied up in court, so she missed hearing about it as well.

"Yeah, I know. Me too," agreed Danny. "Especially this one. But the stuff he gave tracked with what we already knew and never released to the media. You think it's enough to charge Defreitis with the murders?"

"On just the word of Reggie? No. At least not yet," Peck said, and opened one of those small bottled waters that seemed to be popular. Danny never saw any of them at his discount store, so he'd never tried one. Kind of seemed like a rip-off; a swig or two of water at full price? No thanks. He'd stick to his bargain basement water.

"I can corroborate some of what Reggie said; the phone records will show that Defreitis stopped using the phone. And I'll call the fire department dive's team and have them check the 'lake' over at Byrd Park."

"How deep is that lake anyway? It's not much of a lake, is it?" Peck asked.

"Not deep at all. Maybe four feet at its deepest. Only deep enough for those paddle boats. If he did toss it in there, I bet the divers will find it. If he'd thrown it down in the canal, we'd be fucked. That thing is crazy deep and has huge catfish in it," Danny replied.

"Why's he giving us this information, anyway?" Peck asked. "Sentence reduction?"

"You got it," Danny said. "He wants some time knocked off, so he can get out and 'get well'. He is looking like shit. I guess the combination between getting shot then getting nothing but jail food isn't agreeing with him."

"Well, we'll see if anything comes of it. You didn't promise him anything, right?" Peck asked.

"Nope."

"It's getting late tonight," Peck said. "You going to set up the divers first thing in the morning? I don't have a morning docket, so I could swing by and see what happens."

"Yup. I sent a fire department captain I know an email and he said he can have a crew over there around 0800. How's that work for you?" Danny asked.

Before she could answer, Danny got a text from Park:

Call me now

"Gotta go," Danny said, walking out of her office and hitting Park's number. "See ya in the morning."

CHAPTER 38

"That dog is lucky as shit," the patrol officer said, watching Thunder drink some water out of a bowl the medics had brought over. "He took a round right in that doggie bullet proof vest. Going through the SUV door must have slowed it down enough for the vest to stop it," the officer observed.

He was right. Standard ballistic vests wouldn't stop a rifle round; it was too small and moved to fast. Sharon had yanked Thunder out of the SUV and checked him for bleeding holes. The shot had apparently hit him hard enough to knock the wind out of him and he'd been laying there trying to recover. Once he'd heard Sharon voice near his head, he had come back around. She'd unstrapped the vest and ran her hands up and down his flanks checking for any kind of penetrating injury.

By then, the medics were there and had already pronounced the driver dead. They ran over when they saw the commotion by Sharon's SUV. Sharon grabbed Thunder by his snout and held his mouth shut while the medics checked him out a second time. Sharon didn't think he'd snap at them but didn't want to take the chance. Once they gave him a clean bill of health and recommended she run him by the vet when she got a chance, they let her keep the water bowl and went back to their ambulance. The parking lot was a huge crime scene and everyone inside of it would be here awhile.

Sharon had texted Park once everything was under control and she knew that Thunder was ok. He'd texted back for her to call him. She stepped away from the SUV and dialed his number.

"Are you sure you're ok, babe?" Park asked.

Looking around to make sure no one could hear, she said, "Yeah, dad. I'm good. I killed that guy, dad. He tried to shoot up me and a bunch of other cops."

"Damn. Dead, huh? Sure you're ok?"

"Dad? He shot Thunder, ok? If I could kill him again I would. I'm fine with what I did. Trust me," she said.

"Ok but listen. IA's going to get involved in this. Major Crimes is, too. I called Danny and he's going to come out there to check on you while he's 'helping' at the scene. I'd come out there, but I know they won't let me get close to you."

"It's fine, dad," sounding like a teenager to a parent busting her chops. She looked across the lot and saw all the unmarked cars pulling up. "What's Danny driving now, anyway? A bunch of unmarked cars just got here."

"I think he's still driving that piece of shit, lima bean green Crown Vic. Listen to me for a second. You listening?"

"Yes, dad."

"Tell IA what happened, but don't talk to the Major Crimes guys until you get a lawyer from the union with you. IA's just internal policies; they can't give their investigation notes to the Major Crimes guys. IA can't charge you criminally; Major Crimes can. I'm sure it was a justified shoot. But cover your ass, kiddo. Got it?"

"Got it," she said, then hung up. One of the IA detectives had gotten out of the car and was walking over to her. He wandered over to the patrol officer keeping the crime scene roster, identified himself as he showed his badge, then headed her way. "Oh, shit," muttered one of the cops near her. "IA," he said, crossing his arms over his chest.

"Officer Wright?" he asked her, after looking at the nametag sewed onto her dark blue uniform shirt.

"Yep. I'm Officer Wright," she confirmed.

"I'm Det. Lemons. We need to talk."

CHAPTER 39

Danny was in his office watching Sharon's interview live on his computer. She'd have to go upstairs to IA once she got done on the 3rd floor, his offices. When she went up there, he couldn't monitor anymore; IA made sure of that. She'd invoked her Garrity Rights right from the start, just like Park had told her. And just like Danny had told Park to tell her. Basically, Garrity was a protection for employees who *may* face criminal charges as they're doing their jobs. It wasn't only for cops but cops probably got the most benefit from it.

If as a cop you shoot someone, there is the possibility that you could be criminally charged with either an aggravated assault if the person is injured, or with murder if that person dies. Just like any other citizen. As such, just because you're a cop doesn't mean you give up your rights, such as the right to not self-incriminate. So, when a cop invokes Garrity, that cop must tell IA what happened and why the shooting occurred. IA cannot give that statement to the prosecutors and detectives investigating the shooting. When it's time to be interviewed by Major Crimes, the cop who shot someone can invoke the Miranda Rights and ask for a lawyer.

Which is what Sharon did. A police union lawyer came in and he and Sharon spoke privately for about a half an hour. The lawyer decided Sharon was good and agreed to let her talk to the Major Crimes detectives on the condition that he, the lawyer, was present. They were wrapping up the interview now. Danny looked down on the floor at the sound of some low growling and chewing. Thunder was laying on the floor, working on a piece of car tire he'd brought with him from the SUV. Technically Thunder should have been brought to the kennels until Sharon was done with all her interviews. But they'd both been through a lot, so Danny let him chill in the office.

"How you doing, bud?" Danny asked. Thunder ignored him and kept on tugging on the piece of tire. Sharon had left him with his lead on, so Danny could take him out to relieve himself. Danny was tempted to take him up to the 5th floor and let him take a dump right outside of the locked IA offices, but knew there were cameras up there.

He was trying to come up with an alternative plan when he heard footsteps coming down the hall. Thunder stopped chewing and looked up, the hair on his back bristling a bit. Lemons got ready to walk into Danny's office, but stopped short when he saw Thunder. He took a step back, then took another step back when Thunder stood up and gave him a low growl.

"Easy, boy," said Danny, not knowing if Thunder understood the English words (Thunder did but pretended he didn't). Danny picked up the lead and wrapped it once around his wrist, just in case Thunder went after Lemons. "What's that dog doing in here, Detective Jacobs?" Lemons asked. "That's a violation; it's supposed to be kenneled until it's handler is through here. Or left in the SUV."

"First of all, why are you always so fucking formal, Lemons? Just because you're in IA doesn't mean you have act like a dick *all* the time. Most of the guys and gals up there are cool. Lighten up."

Lemons stood in the hall, face turning red, not saying anything. Thunder was still standing there growling at him, but he wasn't tugging on the lead.

"Second, Sharon's car got all shot up, so it's now evidence and being taken to the tow lot. And last, and most important, this officer," nodding at Thunder, "was shot in the line of duty today. You think it would be wise to leave him in a kennel after that traumatic experience?"

Thunder sneezed, then farted loudly.

"See?" Danny said. "Stress."

Lemons turned on his heel and stormed off down the hallway. "Well, Thunder," Danny said. "I've got a feeling I'm going to pay for that. What do you think?"

Thunder thought he'd like to keep chewing at his piece of tire, so that's exactly what he did.

CHAPTER 40

"So, how'd it go?" Park asked Sharon while they sat on Danny's back deck. Danny was out in the yard, flipping burgers on the grill. Thunder was beside him, waiting patiently for any leftover burgers or parts thereof. Danny's cats were staring out the window at his infidelity and vowing to make him pay. The sun had gone down and they'd all decided to meet at Danny's for a late dinner.

"It wasn't bad at all. After what you told me about Lemons, I figured he'd be an asshole. But since that guy shot up a couple of Trooper cars and then shot my dog, I think they were just crossing t's and dotting i's."

"Probably so," Park said. "But watch out who you talk to. And you know you'll probably be out on leave for at least two months, maybe three."

"Yeah, that part's gonna blow. But my sergeant's pretty cool, so I'll still go by the kennels and let Thunder hang out with his K9 pals." She reached into the cooler and pulled out a cold water. She twisted off the top and took a sip, then spit it out. "Goddamn!! What the hell?"

Park laughed. "I told you to never, ever drink anything out of Danny's cooler without looking at the label. Let's see what you got." Park turned on his phone's flashlight and aimed it at the label: *Energybee, organic energy drink, lightly carbonated with a splash of cayenne.*

"Jesus, I think he's trying to kill me," she said.

"Not just you. All of us," Park added as he fished around in the cooler, keeping his fingers crossed.

They all sat around the rickety picnic table on the deck, Danny drinking an Energybee, while Park and Sharon opted for tap water on the rocks. Thunder sat on the floor by Sharon's side, his ears and snout just showing over the top of the table. The burgers had been good, but the buns had been a little hard since they came from the day-old-bread-store. Sharon had tossed one to Thunder, and he kept it in his mouth for a minute or two, *probably to soften it up,* she thought. She should have done the same thing.

"So, was the guy I killed the same dude who robbed Fidelity Bank and got away?" Sharon asked.

"Almost certainly," Danny said. We won't know for sure until all the lab stuff comes back, which will take upwards of six months and maybe more. There was a shit ton of evidence at the bank scene and another cubic shit ton at your scene. Sydney squared and their crew are going to be tied up for days."

Danny took a sip of the Energybee and winced, seeing Sharon and Park give him a smug look. "Ah, smooth," he lied.

"Uh-huh," Park and Sharon said in unison.

"Anyway," Danny said, putting the drink can down on the railing, "We called up to the NYPD and asked that they run your dead guy through their database. Your guy's name is, *was* I should say, Anthony Osbourne. He's definitely got some involvements up there with our known dead guy from the bank. Throw in the New York plates on the car and the rifle and I think we can conclude that the bad guy on the run is no longer on the run. Thanks to you," he said, nodding at Sharon. Sharon nodded back and asked Park, "Did you give Abad a call to let him know?"

"Yep," Park said. "I think it put his mind at ease some, but he's still leaving. He said he lined up a job just outside of Jersey City with one of those smaller Jersey police departments."

"A damn shame," said Danny. "I hate when we lose officers to what amounts to politics and 'optics'."

"I second that," Park said.

"And my vote makes it unanimous. At least out here, right now," stated Sharon. And then to Thunder, "C'mon boy, let's roll." Thunder had edged out into the yard to explore some, but turned and trotted back over to Sharon.

"Ok, guys. Time to start my forced vacation. You two stay safe. And Danny? Get some better drinks." She gave Danny a fist bump, then gave Park a quick kiss on the cheek. Park and Danny watched them go out the side gate, then a minute later heard a truck engine start and recede in the distance.

"Shooting through the windshield was pretty badass," Danny said.

"Yeah."

"She's gonna be just fine, Park. I can feel it," Danny said.

"I sure hope so, brother. I sure hope so."

CHAPTER 41

The next morning, Danny was sitting on the retaining wall that surrounded the lake at Byrd Park. The fire department had pulled up a few minutes after he did. The team leader, Captain Greg Jackson, came over and shook Danny's hand.

"How's it going today, Greg? Ready to find a gun for me?" Danny asked.

"We'll see about that. How long ago do we think it got tossed in the water?"

"Within the last month or so. I think he was driving by on the Boulevard and tossed it out the car window as he was leaving town," Danny said.

"Well, that'll narrow it down some," Jackson replied. "We'll start the search at the side nearest the Boulevard, then work our way out. Might as well make yourself comfortable; this is going to take a while."

"Need me to bring your guys anything?" Danny asked. He'd brought along a spare coffee for Peck, but was hoping Jackson wouldn't take him up in his offer; he didn't necessarily carry a whole dive team's worth of coffee from the shop back over to the lake.

"Nah, we're good. We've got a cooler in the truck. See you soon, I hope."

Danny turned and walked back over to the wall and took a seat. After a few minutes, Peck pulled into the parking lot and walked over. "Ah, coffee. My savior," she said. Danny handed her the cup and she sat beside him to watch and wait.

An hour had gone by and they'd run out of stuff to talk about, so both were looking at their phones. Someone whistled from over near the fire truck and waved Danny and Peck over. As he was walking, he got a text, but he was too excited to look at it right now.

One of the fire guys had surfaced and was flopping his way over to the truck. Correction, based on the curves showing from the dive suit, *she* was flopping her way over to the truck. She made it out of the water and squished over to where Jackson, Danny, and Peck were standing.

"Kae found it, we think," Jackson said, gesturing with his chin to a gun in the diver's gloved hand. "It wasn't too far out," the diver said. "Luckily there wasn't a bunch of trash and shit all around it. Where do you want it?" she asked, holding it down to the side, gloved finger on the slide, not the trigger; not her first time holding a gun.

Danny had gotten a cardboard gun box from Sydney squared before he came to the lake, so he put it on the hood of the fire truck (getting a few nasty looks from the firefighters who were waiting for their turn to go in the water). He pulled a few dry sheets of brown paper towel out of his pocket and lined the gun box with it. "Put it in here, please," Danny asked.

"Want me to make it safe first, since I have gloves on?" the diver asked.

"Nah. I'll let my forensic folks do all the manipulation on it. Hopefully they can get something useful off of it."

The diver shrugged her shoulders and gingerly placed the gun in the box. Danny closed it up and wrote "NOT SAFE" on the outside of the box. He thanked the diver and told Jackson, "I really owe you and your crew, Greg. You guys are the best."

"That's what we do and how we do it," said Greg. "See you on the next one."

Danny turned to walk back to the car when he noticed Peck wasn't beside him. He looked back and saw her talking to one of the divers who had pulled the top of his wetsuit down to waist level. "Peck!! For Christ's sake, come on!!"

She finished her conversation and caught up with Danny. "Way to cock block me, Danny," she said, looking over her shoulder and nearly tripping in the soft grass. She grabbed a hold of Danny's arm to right herself. "I wonder if he saw me grab you and it made him jelly?"

Danny rolled his eyes and said, "Can we concentrate, here? I'm going to get this over to the Sydneys and see what they can tell me."

"Ok, let me know," Peck said, back to business now that she was away from the shirtless firefighter. As she drove off, she honked her horn and both he and the firefighter waved.

He remembered that he'd gotten a text before the gun was found and checked it. It was from his sergeant:

Did you threaten to sic Thunder on Lemons?

Oh boy.

CHAPTER 42

"How were your days off, Shook?" Park asked. They were riding together again, but not because Shook needed more additional training. The problem today was a lack of cars/SUVs to go around. Park, like most old guys, preferred to drive around solo, whereas the younger guys liked teaming up. Shook, however, had more than proven himself in some hairy situations and took criticism well, so Park didn't mind pairing up.

"Oh, not too bad. Didn't do too much. Got caught up in court for most of one of the days off, so that sucked. But I did get almost four hours overtime, so that'll be nice come payday."

Small talk out of the way, Park marked on duty.

"113 to radio?"

"Go ahead, 113," the dispatcher answered.

"We're having MDT problems, so I'm going to mark on the old-fashioned way." Sometimes the computers in the vehicles acted wonky, so officers had to mark on duty over the air, giving their unit number, code number, and vehicle shop number; all the information that was usually transmitted via the MDTs. Park marked on duty, adding Shook's code to his unit, so they were now a two-officer unit.

"Radio copies. And 113, respond to the MLK Market and see the complainant in reference to a parking complaint. Respond code 2; 0715hrs."

"113 copies from the precinct," Park transmitted and drove out of the lot. "Now why the hell is Meredith calling about some parking complaint?" Park wondered aloud.

"She probably wants to show you her tits in person," Shook offered; Meredith had a habit of sending Park nudes via text messages. It had gotten him in trouble on more than one occasion.

"Damn, I hope not," Park said.

"Oh, I don't know," Shook responded. "I think it's a pleasant way to start the day." Park groaned and headed off to see what Meredith wanted.

Park pulled up in front of the market and marked 10-23. Meredith was standing out in front of the store, literally wringing her hands. "Oh, boy," Park said. "This can't be good."

"Goddamn, Park! What took you so long to get here? I called like 20min ago. Shit!"

"Calm down, Meredith. What's going on? The call just read a parking complaint. Someone park in your loading zone or something?" Park asked.

"No, someone's not parked in my loading zone. Jesus. I think there's a dead body in the car behind the building."

Shook started hustling around to the rear of the store, while Park walked with Meredith. "Well, why didn't you say so when you called 911?" Park asked.

Shook was looking into an older, red car that was nosed in to the back of the store. He tried the driver's side door handle, but found it locked. He quickly walked around to the other side, saying to Park, "Looks like someone's in there."

Park keyed up the radio, "113 to radio? Start Fire and medics this way. Male inside a car, not responsive." Then to Shook, "Can you tell if he's breathing?"

"Doesn't smell like he's breathing," Shook said, trying the passenger side door handle; locked.

Park caught a whiff of it too. Once you smell a dead person, you'll always remember the smell. "Ah, 113 to radio? Subject is unconscious and not breathing. Make sure a supervisor copies, please."

"10-4, 113. One male down in a vehicle, unconscious and not breathing. Fire and EMS are on the way in. Supervisor copy?"

"105 copies," Sgt. Rooney said. "Keep me advised, 113."

Shook took his ASP out of its scabbard and extended it out toward the ground. He stepped back from the car to get some swinging distance, then hit the passenger side window with it. The safety glass cracked, then he hit it one more time and it shattered all the way. "Bleaah!" Shook said, backing away further to let the smell dissipate.

Park and Meredith got upwind and Park asked, "So....why didn't you *say* there was maybe a dead guy in a car?" Sirens sounded in the distance and gradually got closer. Shook walked to the side of the store, took the ASP in an overhand grip (like he was going to stab someone) and rammed it against the wall, collapsing the ASP back down to its normal size.

"Because," said Meredith, "I didn't want all this commotion until I knew for sure. You know Amir and I are trying to turn this store into something better than a bodega in a bad neighborhood. Crime scene tape discourages the clientele I'm trying to attract."

Park shook his head, then walked over to the car and peered in. A male about 50 years old was laying prone in the seat, fully dressed with goggles covering his eyes. "Were you guys closed yesterday?" Park asked Meredith.

"Yep," Meredith answered. "Amir and I need to get our swerve on sometimes during normal business hours, so we'll close the store for a day when the mood strikes. There's no fucking like daytime fucking during business hours."

"Watch your language around Shook. He's impressionable. And TMI, by the way."

"I'm not that impressionable," said Shook. Then, "What's that thing on the floor of the passenger side?" pointing at what looked like a small grill.

"Hibachi," Park said. "See the goggles?" Shook nodded. "He put those on because the fumes from the hibachi would hurt his eyes before it killed him. Suicide by hibachi."

"So, he wanted to kill himself, but didn't want his eyes to sting. Classic," said Shook.

"Who can blame him?" Park said. "He'd already made the decision to kill himself. Why make it hurt any more than it has to?"

The sirens winded down and a couple medics walked over to the car. One of them got on her radio and told their dispatch that the fire department could disregard. Within a minute, additional sirens that had been closing in shut off.

"I'll get the tape," Shook said, referring to the yellow crime scene tape. Park tossed him the keys to the car. Meredith saw him getting the roll out of the trunk of the car and started bitching to Park, "Man, c'mon Park! Do you really have to put that up?"

"You know I do, Mer," Park said. Then he turned to Shook and said, "Try to keep most of it in the back, Shook." Shook nodded and began looking for places to tie each end.

"Thanks, Park. You're an ok guy; for a cop," Meredith said.

Park gave her the finger, subtly, then called his supervisor.

CHAPTER 43

"Don't you think I have anything better to do than listen to an IA sergeant gripe to me about one of my detectives threatening one of his detectives?" Major Crimes Detective Sergeant Ryan Dean said. Danny had come back from the lake and was sitting in Dean's office, listening to him gripe.

"I'm at home, trying to relax, then I get a call from the lieutenant, who got a call from the captain, who was contacted by the major after the IA captain called him. See how shit rolls downhill?" Dean asked.

"Looks like it rolled uphill first, then back down," Danny observed.

"Be that as it may, did you threaten Lemons with Thunder? He says you did. If that's the case we've got a problem. Lemons is saying Thunder's vicious and should either be retired or put down."

"That motherfucker!" Danny cursed. "He mentioned *killing* Thunder? I'm gonna go find him and break his neck." Danny stood up to go commit a felony, but Dean blocked his path.

"Ryan, I swear to God, if you get in my way, I'm going to toss you out a window. We've been friends for a long time, but I'll see if you can belly flop on the sidewalk three floors down."

"Sit down and calm the fuck down, Danny," Dean said. "You know Lemons is a dick. But if you used Thunder to threaten him, he's got a valid point."

"I didn't use Thunder to threaten him. Thunder was in my office after he and Sharon got into the shooting at the mall parking lot. He was recuperating while Sharon was getting interviewed. He'd been shot, remember?" Dean nodded, and Danny continued. "Lemons comes into the office and immediately jumps in my shit about why Thunder was there. I told him, and then Thunder got pissed and started growling. That was it. That pussy Lemons backed out into the hallway, then probably ran to tell his supervisor with piss running down his leg."

"Ok. Well, just be aware of what the complaint is. And do NOT, I repeat, NOT approach Lemons or say anything to him about this. It has to go through channels. Got it?" Dean asked.

Danny sat there red faced and fuming for a minute or two, then got himself under control. "Got it."

"Now," Dean continued, shifting gears, "What's the deal with the double?"

"I think we're going to be golden with that gun," Danny said. "Forensics was able to lift some prints off of the bullets that were still in the magazine. And I called up to the Medical Examiner's Office in New York and they did get a bullet out of Bernadette's body. In the next couple of days, a forensic team is going to need to go up there and bring the evidence back here to submit to the lab."

"Peck doesn't just want them to FedEx the stuff to us?" Dean asked, thinking about the expense of sending detectives up to New York just to pick up some bullets and trace evidence.

"No," Danny answered. "She doesn't want to put FedEx in the chain-of-custody. We're going to have enough issues in court without the added one of custody." Chain-of-custody referred to how many hands touch a piece of evidence; the fewer hands, the better.

"Ok. I'll reach out to the forensic supervisor and get them to make the arrangements. It's just a six-hour drive; maybe they could do it in a day," Dean said.

Whatever, Danny thought. *His problem, not my problem.*

"Also, the M.E. up there confirmed the wound location Reggie said, which he got from Defreitis, was accurate. I think once we get the ballistics back, Peck's going to authorize a murder indictment against him."

"Good deal. I'm glad this one's coming together. Ok, keep up the good work. And remember, stay away from Lemons," Dean said.

"Got it; again," confirmed Danny.

"And for God's sake, don't tell Park about Lemons' threat to put down Thunder. He'd tell Sharon and a shit storm would be imminent."

"My lips are sealed," promised Danny.

CHAPTER 44

"That motherfucker said what??!!" Park asked.

"Yep," Danny confirmed. He had gone to the top of the parking deck at HQ and called Park after leaving Dean's office. He made sure that he was facing the door just in case Ryan didn't trust him not to say anything and came outside.

"Over and over that guy is proving to be real douchebag," Park said. "And Sharon said she didn't think he was that bad a guy."

"Well, she was wrong; he is. You're out on the hibachi suicide?" Danny asked.

"Yeah, just waiting on someone from your shop to get here. M.E. investigator's on the way also," Park answered. "Was this hibachi shit on the internet recently? This is like my 3rd one in as many months."

"I'm not sure how it got started," Danny said. "Your people introduced Hari Kari to the world, so I guess whoever invented the hibachi felt left out."

"My *people* aren't Japanese, you racist," Park responded.

"I'm not racist," Danny protested, "I'm culturally curious." Park sneezed into the phone and Danny blessed him. "Anyway, I got to get back inside. The double is picking up steam again and I've got shit to do. By the way, don't mention what Lemons said to Sharon. She's got enough on her mind without worrying about her dog being put down."

"Mum's the word," Park said. "I'll catch up with you later."

* * *

"He said *what*??!!" Sharon exclaimed after Park told her. "Why'd Danny use Thunder to threaten him?" she asked.

"Danny didn't use Thunder to threaten him; Lemons just got his panties all twisted up in a bunch."

"I swear, if they try to take Thunder from me, all that's going to be left of them is eyeballs and broken teeth littering the floor." Thunder looked up from his tire piece and gave an enthusiastic *woof* to let her know he agreed and to count him in.

"They're not going to take him; don't sweat it. Lemons was just being an asshole. His natural state," Park replied. "Listen, don't tell Danny I told you. He told me in confidence. Ok?"

"Ok, but he's the *first* one to get it if they even look at Thunder sideways. Love ya." She hung up and Park walked back over to the hibachi car.

Danny felt his phone buzz in his shirt pocket and checked out the screen: a text from Sharon. It was whole bunch of eyeball and teeth emojis, plus a few middle finger emojis thrown in for good measure. Danny got the middle fingers, but what was the deal with the eyeballs and teeth? He shrugged his shoulders and got back to work.

CHAPTER 45

Park was off for the next couple of days and the original plan had been to do some more work on Danny's deck. What had started out as shoring up some of the weaker (on the railing) had morphed into a full-blown redo, with a roof added to the plans when Danny had seen one in a magazine. But with Danny rolling on the double, Park had some free time. And whenever he had free time and the weather was cooperating, he rolled out the motorcycle. Tugging on his jeans (a little tight) and his steel-toed riding boots (fit just right), he backed his cruiser out of the garage and got on the road.

Virginia State Police Trooper Erin Garcia was enjoying a fairly uneventful morning on the stretch of I-95 that ran through Richmond, Henrico, and Hanover. She'd worked up in Northern Virginia for a few years right after she'd graduated from the academy and had finally gotten the transfer she'd requested months ago. NoVa was a nightmare when it came to traffic and congestion. She'd made trips up north to her home state of Delaware, and NoVa was almost always the only place she hit nuclear traffic congestion. Driving through it on the occasional trip home was one thing; working accidents as a Trooper was a whole new category of miserable. The pay was higher because of the cost of living in the suburbs of DC, but it wasn't worth it to her. She preferred the less busy section of the Richmond area. She'd found a nice townhouse in northern Hanover that was right off the highway and right in her price range.

So far this morning she'd nabbed one speeder and handled one non-reportable accident (no injuries and only about $500.00 damage). After clearing from the accident, she pulled off the highway to grab an energy drink and a cup of ice from a convenience store; today was going to be a hot one.

Park truly loved riding the motorcycle. Despite hearing about fatal accidents involving motorcycles, he felt 'throttle therapy' was a real thing. He'd see a news report about a motorcycle fatality, then go on a ride just to make sure he didn't get psyched out. He'd only worked one motorcycle accident in his career and that guy didn't die, though he did go over a guardrail and drop a few stories into a thicket below the highway. Park remembered being on scene and one of the firefighters saying, "This guy looks like a pretzel," and the guy responding, "I can hear you." That was a teachable moment in discretion and keeping your voice low for first responders.

Actually, that incident kept Park away from highways as often as he could. But he liked taking the twisty back roads. He'd been on the back roads for about an hour now and the ride, his bladder, and his age told him it was time for a pit stop. He came to an intersection and saw a convenience store right near the highway junction. Looking left and right, he took the turn and motored on into the parking lot. As he was pulling in, a Trooper was pulling out. The sun was glinting off the car's windows, so he couldn't tell if he knew the Trooper of not. As a city cop, he didn't have much interaction with the Troopers since his precinct wasn't all that close to any highway. Every summer, the Troopers would ride with Richmond officers for a gun initiative, so Park would see them then. And last summer, a Trooper was shot and killed during the initiative, so Park got to meet a lot of them during the subsequent investigation and lock down of the neighborhood in which he was killed.

Regardless, the Trooper drove out of the lot and Park decided to put some gas in his bike before relieving himself. Priorities.

Garcia pulled out of the parking lot just as a motorcycle was pulling in. She loved the looks of motorcycles, especially the big cruisers, but those things were death machines as far as she was concerned. She'd worked numerous accidents with bikes, and most were fatal. Her guys, the Troopers in the motor unit, loved them though. *To each his own*, she thought, and waited to make a left turn onto the 95 North entrance ramp.

Park topped off his tank, tapped the tip against the hole, then racked the hose back on the pump. He screwed the cap back on his tank and pocketed the keys. Leaving his helmet hung over the handlebar mirror, he heard the Trooper's car accelerate onto the highway as he walked inside the store to find the bathroom.

Garcia had made her left onto the entrance ramp when she saw an SUV with blacked out windows hauling ass on 95. It wasn't a police SUV; they were usually Fords or Chevys. This one looked to be a Mitsubishi and it was easily doing 100mph. She hit her lights and siren, pressed down on the accelerator, and merged onto the highway, adrenaline starting to flow.

* * *

Park heard the siren whoop in the distance as he was walking out of the bathroom. Just as a siren calls a sailor, a siren calls a cop. Park wondered if it was the Trooper he saw leaving the parking lot. It was receding into the distance, so he walked over to the drink cooler to grab something to drink when a case of bear claws caught his eye.

Just as fast as the adrenaline hit her, it ebbed when the SUV pulled right over once she got behind it. Hell, it even used its blinker to go across two lanes of traffic from the left lane to the far-right shoulder. She made sure that she left a good two-car length space between her car and the SUV. She positioned her car to the left of the SUV, giving herself a safe path from traffic to walk from her car to the SUV. She cranked her wheel hard to the left so in the event of a gunfight, the wheel would provide some cover to her legs and feet. She did all these actions without giving them much thought; it was how she was trained. Her instructors had told her academy class that people wanted to kill cops; never forget that and do your best to go home at the end of every shift.

Leaving her emergency lights on, she checked the license plate on her MDT and found that the SUV was not wanted, and the owner didn't have any warrants on file. And as a bonus, the owner was even licensed; truly an aberration. She called the traffic stop in to her dispatch and approached the

SUV from the passenger's side, hand resting on her gun, her dash-cam rolling.

She rapped on the window with her left hand, and after a brief hesitation, it rolled down. She peered in and saw two males in the front; the back was empty. "My name is Trooper Garcia with the Virginia State Police. I pulled you over for two reasons: number one, excessive speed back there near the on-ramp. Number two, the tint on your windows is too dark."

"Son of a bitch!!" said the driver. "I knew this tint was too dark. That's what I get for going to a budget place."

"I need your license and registration, sir," Garcia said. He asked permission to reach into the glove compartment for the information and Garcia nodded. But kept her hand on her gun.

"Let me get your ID, too, sir," Garcia said to the passenger.

"Why do you need my ID? I'm not driving."

"Don't be an asshole, just give her your license," the driver said to the passenger. "Fine," he grumbled and raised up on an ass cheek to fish his wallet out of his back pocket. "Here, take it. I'm clean," he said, handing it to her.

"Thank you, gentlemen," she said, "I'll be right back." She walked backwards a few steps keeping her eye on the SUV until she came abreast of her cruiser. She got back in her car and checked both through the MDT; both clean. She let her dispatcher know that she was 10-4 and started writing the summonses.

Park went back to the bathroom to wash the sticky from the bear claw off his hands. He was initially going to have a soda, but since he ate the claw, he figured water would be easier on his midsection. Then he passed by the chocolate milk; well, calcium was good for you too.

He walked back out to his bike and put on his helmet and gloves. Full bike, full belly. He cranked it up and thought about which way to go. He knew there were some more twisty roads beyond the entrance ramp of the highway. Then he remembered seeing the Trooper accelerate down the ramp and hearing the siren whoop. He decided he'd jump on the highway to make sure the Trooper was ok, then get off on the next exit and have some more fun on the back roads.

Decision made, he put his blinker on, took a right then a left onto the entrance ramp.

Garcia finished both summonses and put her pen back in her pocket. She kept a hand exerciser in the center console and gave it ten squeezes on each hand. She was a boxer and liked to keep her muscles activated. She looked in her rearview mirror to make sure traffic was clear, then stepped out of her car. She didn't like walking up to a car with a summons book in her hand, so she motioned to the driver to come back to her. She put the summons book on the hood of her car and stepped back, letting the driver walk by her and stand facing the hood. She was right-handed and stayed to his right as she explained the summonses to him. There was a lot of tractor trailer traffic, so she had to keep her voice raised.

"The first summons is for the speeding. I could have written you for reckless, but since you're polite and cooperative, I just wrote it for 15 over." The driver wasn't happy about it, but he signed the summons.

"The second one is for your tint. Like I said, it's too dark. You're going to need to get that fixed or else you'll keep getting pulled over."

"But that's bullshit!" the driver griped. "The company that did the tint said it was ok. I paid them. Why should I get the ticket?"

"Because you're driving the car and it's your responsibility," she said. "Bring your receipt to court with you."

"But that's fucked up," the driver persisted. "Why should *I* get a ticket for something *they* did??"

Garcia was starting to lose her patience; *what was so hard to understand?* A motorcycle approached as she began to explain it to him again; with her body turned toward him and away from the SUV, she didn't hear the passenger get out of the SUV and come up behind her.

Park saw the bright emergency lights of the Trooper's car on the right shoulder about 400 yards ahead. He put his blinker over and eased into the right lane. The other cars coming up on the Trooper's car had moved to the center lane, following Virginia law. Since Park was on a motorcycle, he took up less space in the lane, so he presented less of a danger to a Trooper on the side of the road than a full-sized vehicle did. Plus, he wanted to get close enough to make sure the Trooper was ok.

As he was coming abreast of the car, he saw that the Trooper had a guy out of the SUV, signing some summonses on the hood of the Trooper car. It looked like the Trooper was engaged in a conversation with him, with her back turned away from the SUV. As he passed by, his heart raced as he saw another male coming up behind the Trooper. He was looking in his rearview mirror as the male behind the Trooper wrapped his arm around her throat and pulled her from Park's view.

CHAPTER 46

"No way in fucking hell!" Reggie said. "There's no way I'm going to testify against that guy. Uh-uh. Nope." Reggie was sitting in the contact visitation room down at the Justice Center at a table across from Danny and Peck. And he was clearly not happy.

"Me testifying was never part of the deal," he continued.

"Are you fucking crazy?" Peck asked. "Who the fuck do you think you're talking to?" Danny just sat back and watched; apparently, he was playing good cop to Peck's bad cop. Reggie looked back and forth between Danny and Peck, clearly confused.

"Um, I'm talking to you?" making it sound like a question.

"No, you're not talking to me like that. Try again," Peck responded.

"Try again, how?" Reggie asked.

"With some respect, asshole. For starters."

"Ok. Um, sorry. But I'm not testifying. Out of the question," Reggie insisted.

"Oh yeah? Then how do you think you're going to get any kind of reduced time, genius? You think you give us some information and we just say, 'Gee, thanks, Reggie. Great job. As a reward, you get to go home now.' Is that what you think, idiot?" Peck mocked.

"Why are you calling me names, lady? Damn, detective, what the fuck?" Reggie whined.

"I said, show me some fucking respect!!" Peck yelled, slamming both hands down on the table hard enough to make Reggie and Danny jump. Before Reggie could respond, she said, "You are going to testify to what you told Danny. You're going to get up on the stand and look at me when I ask you questions. Then you're going to look at the defense attorney when he or she asks you questions, then you go home early. See how easy that is?"

"But that guy's going to kill me if I do that," Reggie answered.

"How's he going to kill you Reggie when he's in jail, huh? He fucking killed two people. You think he's getting out for good behavior? He's fucking *through*. Life plus 50 years," Peck said.

"You promise he'll get found guilty and get all those years?"

"No, because I have to rely on you for some of it and you still might fuck it up even when you do testify. Notice how I said *when* you do, not *if* you do?" Reggie nodded his head, maybe unconsciously. Danny did too.

"I can promise you this; if you don't testify, he's going to get out before you and he knows he told you what happened. I bet he's got a long memory and is patient. He'll go online and see when you're scheduled to be released, then wait for you. If you're lucky, you'll only wind up dead in the back of a car. I'd bet he tortures you first to see if you told anyone. And you did. And you'll break. I wouldn't want to die like that. Would you, detective?"

Danny shook his head; he most certainly did not.

"So, what's it going to be Reggie? Never mind; I already know the answer. You're going to testify, then you'll get out early and he goes to jail for the rest of his miserable life. C'mon detective, let's roll." And she picked up her folder and tugged on the door to leave the room. It would have been a dramatic exit, but the door was locked from the outside and she had to hit a buzzer and wait for the unlock. After about a minute, the door buzzed, and the lock disengaged. Danny looked at Reggie, shrugged his shoulders, and followed Peck out.

CHAPTER 47

Garcia was in trouble. She had been so focused on the asshole complaining about his tint, she'd lost situational awareness for a split second and let the passenger get behind her. He'd wrapped his arm around her neck and pulled her off her feet. She put her right hand on her gun and rammed her left elbow back into his midsection. He took the blow and kept tugging her backwards, away from the highway and to the side of her car, shielding what was happening from passing traffic.

The passenger behind her tried to throw her on the ground by yanking her sideways, but she kept her legs out straight, then kicked against her police car. She elbowed him again, but it was like elbowing a wall. She raised her foot up, then stomped down on his foot, but he was wearing steel toe shoes; no effect. She began to get worried.

Park had seen the Trooper get pulled behind her car and frantically looked for an exit ramp or a break in the guardrail where he could do a U-turn and get back to the Trooper. No breaks that he saw, but he saw the exit ramp sign ahead; 1

mile. He twisted the throttle all the way and made it to the exit ramp in under a minute. Now to get turned around.

Garcia was feeling herself weaken, but leaned forward and then flung her head back right into the passenger's nose. She felt it crunch and he immediately screamed, "You fucking bitch!!" She got away from him, trying to increase her distance and pull her gun, but the driver kicked her in the side of her knee, breaking something inside of it. She gasped and fell against the side of her car. She stood to get her bearings and defend herself, when the driver punched her in the throat, knocking her down on the ground. Gagging, she put one hand on the ground, refusing to go down when the passenger with the broken nose stomped on her hand, breaking her fingers. *I'm going to die here*, she thought....

Park took the exit ramp, but when he got to the top he realized that there was no re-entry point at this exit. *Motherfucker!!* he thought. He looked left, then right, and then back down the ramp he'd just used. *Fuck it*, he thought and turned around, heading down the exit ramp and picking up speed. *Hold on baby*, he thought. *Just hold on.*

* * *

Garcia didn't think she could hold on anymore. She wasn't even sure where she was or who she was. After the passenger crushed her fingers, he lifted her against the car by her throat and punched her in the stomach. Her vest took part of the blow, but it still doubled her over. She wound up on her back and he straddled her, raining punches down on her face. It was like the two assholes were tag-teaming in; first the passenger, then the driver, then the passenger again. She began to lose consciousness, but he still punched in the face over and over again. The last thing she heard before everything went dark and the pain went away was the sound of a motorcycle engine getting closer and closer. Then nothing.

* * *

Park had driven on the shoulder of the highway, southbound in the northbound lanes. He could see one guy on top of the Trooper, steadily punching her in the face and head. The other guy, the driver, was watching the beating, but as Park got closer, turned to look at the motorcycle hauling ass towards him. When Park was about 50 yards away, he slowed the big bike, downshifted, turned the handlebars to the left and hit the rear brakes. The bike went over on its left side, dumping Park on the pavement in a more or less controlled slide; his riding jeans doing a pretty good job of protecting his thighs and ass as he slid behind the bike.

The 800-plus pound bike kept sliding, hitting the driver in the legs and breaking both at the knee. The driver fell forward over the skidding bike, then got caught under it as it flipped over three times before resting on an embankment.

The guy on top of the Trooper heard the crash and turned around as Park was coming to the end of his slide. He charged at Park, running full on. Park had just gotten himself to his feet when the guy hit him broadside, nearly knocking Park back down on his ass. But Park was a big man and had been in many street fights over the course of his career. The guy drove his head into Park's gut and wrapped both arms around his waist. But that was all he could do with him. Park bent at the waist and wrapped his arms around the guy's back. Both men trying to gain the advantage. Park looked over and saw the Trooper motionless on the ground, blood covering her face, fingers mangled on her left hand, bent at all the wrong angles. He began to see red.

Most fights Park got into weren't personal; the bad guy was just trying to get away. In those cases, Park was just subduing the guy with enough force to get him, or her, into custody.

Not this time. This fucker had tried to kill a police officer. Park leaned down further and squeezed his arms together with all his might, getting his face closer to the back of the guy's head. When he was right against the side of his head, he bit down on his ear and tore into like an animal. The guy twisted his head side to side, trying to get loose from Park's teeth. He pummeled Park's side and back, but Park didn't feel it. Park drove his knee up into the guy's face hard enough to lift him up off of the ground. Then he did it again. The second one hit him hard enough for him to cough blood out onto Park's knee. Park let go of him with his left hand and drove his elbow straight down into the guy's spine; not caring if he broke it or not.

The guy went down on one knee, trying to catch his breath. "Get up," Park commanded, quietly. Nearly a whisper. "Get up so I can kill you, you cowardly motherfucker." Park stood over him, hands clenching, blood dripping from his chin from where he had bitten through the guy's ear. "Get up, get up, get up." The guy took a few more breaths, then looked at Park. He fell back on his ass and held both hands out to be cuffed. Park walked behind him, grabbed him by the collar and dragged him over to the wrecked motorcycle which was on top of the wrecked man. Park took the set of cuffs he always carried with him off his belt and cuffed both men together, running the cuff through the steel motorcycle frame.

He went over to the Trooper, saw her face and said, "Oh, no,no,no.....c'mon baby girl. C'mon Trooper. Hang in there, c'mon baby." She was breathing, but it sounded labored. Her shoulder mic had been ripped off her shoulder and lay broken feet away from her. He opened her patrol car door and grabbed the radio mic from its base:

"This is RPD Officer Park, calling in a mayday, Trooper down for one of your Troopers. We're at exit 98, 95-Northbound. Radio copy?"

"Radio copies stand by." Park heard the tones go out over the VSP frequency, then the dispatcher was back on the air.

"Officer Park, what is the Trooper's condition?"

"She's unconscious and barely breathing," Park relayed. "Severe trauma to the head, body, and left hand. Tell EMS to step it up."

"10-4, Officer Park. They're on the way. Suspect info?"

"Both in custody," Park said. "Have your uniformed guys be advised I'm at the Troopers side, so don't bum rush me when they arrive. I'm wearing blue jeans and a yellow vest; bad guys are handcuffed to my wrecked motorcycle."

"10-4, Park. Units less than a minute out."

Park left the mic on the car seat and sat beside the Trooper, hand gently on her left arm. "Hang in there, honey. Help's on the way." That's when he noticed that her right hand was still on her holster, keeping her gun secure. "You're safe now, Trooper," Park comforted her, a catch in his voice, as the sound of sirens started getting closer. "I'm a cop."

CHAPTER 48

"You did what???!!" Danny asked Park. It was about three hours since the incident on the highway. Garcia, (Park had found out her name by looking at her name tag while waiting for the cavalry and medics to respond), had been transported by Med-Flight to the Trauma Center at the university. There had been a few tense moments when the responding Troopers pulled up and saw Park beside their severely injured Trooper. Luckily one of the 1st Troopers there was an old guy like Park and was able to allow cooler heads, namely his, prevail. He also had to remind the young Troops that the dash cams and body cams were rolling, so make sure the prisoners received adequate medical care, then plan to get them transported to a hospital. But not with Garcia.

The older Trooper assured Park that once the prisoners were extricated from his motorcycle, it would be returned to him. The original ambulance that had responded for Garcia, took Park instead. They brought him in to the ER and took a few x-rays and CAT scans (right after he wrecked his bike and before the guy attacked him, he'd thrown his helmet to the ground), so they wanted to make sure he didn't have a brain bleed. Once they were satisfied that nothing was broken on the inside, they tended to his outside; namely the road rash he'd gotten sliding across the pavement after his bike. He'd slowed down enough before he dropped it to avoid his skin being flayed off, but he did have some semi-deep abrasions on his hands, thighs, and ass that needed to be cleaned. Which was how Danny found him when he walked back into the examination room. After the required ribbing about his bare ass sticking up in the air, then Park's retort, Park had told him what happened.

"So, where in the hell did you learn how to slide a motorcycle into a guy? Did they stop teaching that class prior to me joining the department?" Danny asked.

"Just seemed like the right thing to do. Owwww! Shit!!" Park screeched.

"Sorry," said the nurse. "I'm trying to get all the little stones out. You don't want them to get infected, you know."

"Don't take out the little stones under his little dick," Danny said. The nurse ignored this and said to Park, "I think I got them all out of your thigh and ass cheeks. I checked, and I didn't see any near the hole." Which caused Danny to laugh out loud.

Park threw a vomit bucket at him, making Danny jump back like he'd stepped on a live wire. "Gross Park!! That's not funny!!" The nurse rolled his eyes and left the room.

"So anyway," Danny said as Park rolled over onto the side that hadn't been mildly shredded, giving Danny another shot of his ass. Danny made gagging noises, then continued, "Garcia is out of the woods. You did good by turning her on her side, so the blood could stay out of her throat; that's what would have killed her. Between her throat being swollen from the punch, plus all the bleeding from her face, she would have drowned in her blood for sure."

"Any broken bones in her face? I know her left hand was all fucked up," Park asked.

"Yeah, she's got a broken orbital bone and a broken jaw. Three of the fingers of her left hand got mangled pretty good too." Danny handed Park the loose-fitting clothes he'd grabbed from Park's house after he got the call that he was in the ER.

"The good news," Danny continued, "Is all those broken bones are going to heal. She's got a few cracked ribs, but she should be good to go in 8 months to a year. You did real good, Park. Real good."

Park shrugged the compliment off and lowered his voice. "I was *this* close to killing both of them, Danny. No shit, holding up a thumb and forefinger an inch apart, *this* close."

"That's because you're a good man, Park. Me?" Danny looked him right in the eye and squeezed Park's fingers together, closing the inch gap. "I would have killed them both."

★ ★ ★

Danny left to go back to the office, so Park decided to go check in on Garcia. They had moved her from the ER over to a room in the main part of the hospital; luckily not the CCU (Critical Care Unit), so that was good news for her chances of recovery. He got turned around trying to get to the actual main hospital and had to get directions from a volunteer at the main entrance, then some more directions from someone in scrubs who was hanging out in one of the hallways. When he finally made it to the right floor, he saw a sea of the blue/grey uniforms of the Troopers who came to check on their injured sister.

Like most cops, and maybe even more so, the Troopers protected their own, even in a hospital. Park hadn't taken three steps toward her room when a big Trooper with a birthmark on the side of his face held up a hand for Park to stop. "Help you?" he asked, though his voice and manner said otherwise.

Before Park could respond, the older Trooper who was at the scene shouldered 'birth mark' aside and said, "Fellas, this is Officer Park. He's the *guy*." Just like that the tension was gone and all the Troopers surrounded Park, shaking his hand and clapping him on the back. "Ok, ok, give him some air. C'mere, Park. Follow me."

Park followed him to one of the vacant family rooms and closed the door halfway. "I'm Jim Bombay. I don't think I ever told you my name." They shook hands and Park said, "One of our detectives told me how she's doing. So, the docs think she's going to make a full recovery?"

"That's what we're hearing from her family," Bombay confirmed. "The staff is only letting us go in one at a time. She's not awake yet, but her breathing seems better. Want to go in and see her?"

"No, I'll let her rest," Park said. "How long did it take to get her family here?"

"They live up in Fairfax, so we sent two Troopers screaming up 95, going about 120. They picked them up and got them back within the hour."

"You guys ever find out why those fuckers attacked her?" Park asked.

"Well, the one guy who had the unfortunate 'accident' with your motorcycle, the driver of the car, is still unconscious. The other guy, the passenger? He's not saying anything. He didn't have any warrants on him, car wasn't stolen or involved in any crime we know about. So, it may stay a mystery. But you know what? Who cares? They did it, you fucked them up and put them in the hospital, next they're going to jail. State Police owes you, Park."

"You guys don't owe me anything. I'm just glad she's going to be ok. I'll come back and check on her in a few days."

They shook hands and exchanged cards. As Park was walking out, he said, "You may be getting a call from our IA in reference to the force used on those guys. If you do, can you give me a heads-up, so they don't catch me off guard?"

"We've got that covered, Park. Go home and take it easy."

* * *

"This is Detective Lemons with the Richmond Police Department calling for Investigator Conyers."

"Hold please, detective. I think he's at his desk. Putting you through."

"This is Investigator Conyers. Can I help you?"

"Yes, Investigator. My name is Detective Lemons with Richmond IA. I'm calling about a use of force incident involving one of our off-duty officers: Chester Park."

"What use of force incident?" Conyers asked.

"Um, the one on the highway? Where one of your Troopers was injured? Our officer put two victims in the hospital?"

"Victims?" said Conyers. "The only victim was Trooper Garcia."

"I meant the victims of our officer's use of force," explained Lemons.

"Don't know what you're talking about, Lemongrass. One of Garcia's assailants was struck by Park's motorcycle, which was totaled by the way. The other guy was injured in the assault on Garcia. Your officer rendered aid to Garcia after she was assaulted."

"My last name is Lemons, with an 's'. There must be some mistake. Surely you have dash camera footage or BWC that I can look at."

"We have both. However, it has been reviewed and is strictly for investigative purposes. And this is a State Police investigation. If and when we need assistance from the IA section of the Richmond Police Department, you'll be the first or second to know. Now, I need to get back to work, Lemonade. Drive safely: clickit or ticket. Goodbye."

CHAPTER 49

"You really bit some guy's ear off?" Shook asked as they were getting situated in the car after morning roll call. It had been two weeks since the incident on the highway and the story had been told and retold countless times. One version had Park chewing off both ears, then swallowing them. Another version said that he'd kept one as a souvenir. Still another had him doing a backflip off the motorcycle just before it took out the bad guy, then doing a hero landing, coming down on one knee with his head bowed (this one was his favorite).

"Just part of it," Park replied. He checked the lights on the marked SUV, then tooted the siren and airhorn; all functioning.

"How's your, um, injured area?" Shook asked, trying to see if Park was favoring one ass cheek over the other.

"My road rash is fine, Shook. Goddamn, are you my mother?"

"Just checking partner," Shook said, by now used to Park's grumpiness.

"Well, enough with the checking. I want to go to the hospital and see Garcia. She's going home later today, and I don't want to miss seeing her."

"Man, she's a beauty. Strong, too. Did you see those photos in her room of her boxing? Bad ass and smoking hot." Shook had gone with Park to see her last week and checked out some of the boxing photos that her parents had brought and left around the hospital room.

"Watch yourself, Shook. Last time we went, there were about ten Troopers about the size of tractors watching over her. You really want to put the moves on her with the threat of imminent destruction hovering around?"

"Danger makes life worth living, Park. That's why we do what we do. I think I'm going to ask her out."

Park shook his head as he saw Officer Carl Bailey come jogging out of the precinct. Bailey had been shot a little over a year ago and was finally back on full duty, with seemingly no ill effects of having been shot. Physically, that is. Time would tell if the same could be said about mentally.

"Hey, Park? Sarge needs you back inside for a minute," Bailey said, then turned around and jogged back inside. Park shook his head; these young guys were always jogging everywhere. They needed to watch that great cop movie where the older cop tells his younger partner about a bull and some cows. Park got himself out of the SUV and made his way inside the precinct.

***

When Park got inside, everyone was still sitting at their desks in the roll call room, leading Park to believe that something was up. Ordinarily the troops couldn't get out of roll call fast enough; to get away from the sergeant and/or to get to breakfast. Today, they were all sitting there facing front, hands together on the desks in front of them.

"There's the man of the hour," said Sgt. Rooney. "C'mon in and have a seat, here, Park. Right up front."

"I'd rather not," Park said. "I've got shit to do and I'm sure calls are backing up."

"You can spare a few minutes. The only calls pending are the bullshit ones. If a hot one comes in, we'll roll. And Trooper Garcia isn't scheduled to get out for another hour. Speaking of which, good luck with that Shook, you're going to need it."

"Thanks, sarge," Shook muttered from the back of the room, face turning bright red.

"But I digress," Rooney continued. "Park?" indicating an empty chair at the front. Park sighed and grumbled, but made his way to the front of the room and had a seat in the chair.

"Now, you'll probably be getting some kind of medal, or citation, or other 'Atta-boy' from the much-revered Virginia State Police." A smattering of boos and hisses from the platoon, many of whom had been pulled over by Troopers for speeding while off-duty. Hell, one officer had been pulled over in a marked vehicle, while working, and *in uniform*!

"Since you were off-duty, the only thing you're liable to get from our HQ is a founded IA complaint, courtesy of Det. Lemons." More enthusiastic boos from the audience. "But," Rooney continued, "Your platoon got together and bought you a present that we think represents your accomplishments on that morning. Anderson?"

Anderson came to the front of the room, carrying a package that had been gift wrapped with crime scene tape. He held it out at arm's length while another officer or two made trumpet noises, then presented the gift to Park. Anderson retreated backwards, head bowed in a grand gesture, then promptly tripped over a go-bag someone had left on the floor.

"Officer down!........again!" someone said, making reference to Anderson's shooting last year. Anderson popped back up, dusted himself off, and took another bow before sitting down.

"Open your gift, Park," Rooney said. Park pulled his knife from his pocket and hit the button, shooting the blade out the front of the handle. "Is that shit legal?" someone said from the back. Park ignored her and began slicing the tape away from his package. "A modern-day Samurai," someone observed. "He's not from Japan, you racist," another officer said. "Oh, right. I'm the one from Japan," the first officer responded. "But Park's half-black, too," said the first officer.

"Both of you guys shut up," Rooney said. Then "And Oguri, keep your anti-Asian comments to yourself."

"Hai!" Oguri responded.

"We hope you like it, Park," said Rooney. "We figured you would, after what you did to that guy on the highway..."

Park had gotten through the third and final layer of tape and could smell a bacony scent. He pulled out the bag and found a sack of pig ears, dog treats, that you can buy from the pet stores. Park blushed, then started laughing as the room exploded in applause.

CHAPTER 50

"Hey Cindy, it's Danny. Guess what?"

"I know I was sleeping, that's what," Cindy said, sounding groggy *and* grumpy.

"It's like 10:30 in the morning," Danny said. "You keeping drone hours now?" Danny asked.

"Fuck off, Danny. I had an extradition from Philly and didn't get to bed until 0900. So that puts my sleep deficit in the critical zone. What do you want?"

"Well, we got Defreitis, part two," Danny said. "Except this time, the warrant is for use of a firearm in the commission of a felony, to be upgraded to a double homicide indictment in a few weeks."

"Oh yeah?" Cindy said, sounding more awake and more interested. She may be grumpy when she's lacking sleep, but the hunt for a murderer always gets her blood pumping.

"Oh yeah. You remember that prick Reggie from last year? The guy who caused all that drama, then got shot by a would-be robber? Well, Defreitis actually told Reggie what he did."

"Unbelievable," said Cindy, rolling out of bed and stretching out her back. "He going to testify?"

"Yup," Danny said. "Peck convinced him that it would be in his best interest to testify, and if he didn't, he'd serve his full sentence *and* maybe get killed by Defreitis when he gets out."

"Damn," Cindy said, "An offer he can't refuse. So, the warrant is on file and you already emailed me the wanted poster and the Marshals form?" she asked. The Marshals form was paperwork with all the pertinent information of the wanted person. It included phone numbers, addresses (current and previous), any kind of vehicle they drove, and family or associates.

"Yes, and yes," Danny advised. "And if you're ok with it, I'd like to be there when you pick him up. Peck's put in a lot of work on this one and wants to see him when you cuff him. I'll make sure that we stay out of the way."

"Ok. On it. 'Bye." Cindy hung up.

CHAPTER 51

"You ready to get out of here, Garcia?" Park asked, once he and Shook entered Garcia's room. "You fucking know it," she responded. All the pictures her folks had brought to the room were gone, along with other items people had brought her; a bottle of creatine powder, a case of 5hr energy shots, protein bars, some hand wraps for the heavy bag, and a bunch of police patches from other jurisdictions. The only thing left was a vase of wilted flowers, sitting in the window.

"Your face is still all lopsided," Park observed. "So's yours," she chided. "But mine'll go back to normal; yours is stuck like that," she continued, causing Shook to laugh out loud.

"Ever find out who sent you the flowers?" Park asked, eyeing Shook suspiciously.

"No idea," she said, jamming some of her clothes in a black and blue canvass gym bag. "I guess the tag fell off, or someone took it off. Maybe it went to the wrong room. I mean, who'd send a cop flowers?"

"Excellent question," Park asked, catching the flush on Shook's face. "I'm sure you don't, but do you need a ride home? Shook and I are 10-7 and can give you a lift."

"Nah, I'm good. My platoon is coming by to give me a ride."

She finished packing up and caught Park looking at her. "Are you looking at my ass, Park?"

"Not even a little. Just your crooked face," Park said. "Just amazed at seeing how well you're moving. My shit still hurts."

She laughed and said, "That's because you're like 20 years older than me. But other than my hand," she held up her left hand, which was still in a hard cast and would be for 6 more weeks, "I feel pretty good. My face is still a little swollen from the beating, but the breaks aren't as bad as they thought. Another few months, I'll be back on the road."

A siren sounded outside, and she looked out the window. "That's my ride."

"Why didn't they come upstairs?" Shook asked. "I thought they'd carry you out on their shoulders or something."

"Because I told them not to. I'm walking out of here, no fanfare." She shouldered her bag and walked up to Park. "Thanks for saving my ass out there, Park. I owe you one." Then she kissed him on the cheek.

As she walked by Shook, she held out her hand to shake. When he grabbed it, she pulled him in and whispered, "And thanks for the flowers," giving his ass a squeeze and walking out the door. He opened his hand and found a crumpled piece of paper with her phone number on it. Shook was in love.

CHAPTER 52

"Can I get double chicken with that? Guacamole, too. On the side?" Danny was in line at one of his favorite Mexican restaurants. He'd gotten caught up on most of his paperwork for the double and updated Mrs. Oliver, Bernadette's mother on getting a felony warrant for Defreitis. She'd been calling him nearly every day for updates. Bernadette was her only daughter and she was absolutely heartbroken. She lived in New Jersey and felt completely isolated from the investigation. Danny felt awful for her and spoke to her as often as he could.

Troy's wife, on the other hand, couldn't seem to care less what was going on in the investigation. Danny had only spoken with her a few times, though not for lack of trying; every time he called her, she acted as if she couldn't be bothered with any updates. Eventually he just stopped trying and focused on Bernadette's mom.

"That'll be $12.50," said the cashier. *Shit!* thought Danny. Most of the time the employees gave him a first responders discount. Not today, though. Full price; that was going to hurt. He paid up and walked over to one of the booths in the corner. Like most cops, he didn't like having his back exposed, so preferred to eat facing the door. He sprinkled some hot sauce on the burrito bowl and had the fork dug in and ready to dig in when his phone rang: Cindy.

"Hey, Cindy. What's up?"

"We've got eyes on him. Go get Peck and mount up."

Danny, who may have had a little crush on the prosecutor, said, "Let me finish my lunch and then I'll roll on over. Where are you?"

"By the time you finish your lunch it'll be all over and he'll be in custody. He's down here in Shockoe Bottom at one of the food joints. No line, so he'll probably be in and out. We'll take him once he leaves the area. Up to you." Cindy hung up before Danny could respond.

Danny looked at his full price burrito bowl, then at his phone, then back to his burrito bowl. Sighing, he put down his fork and called Peck.

CHAPTER 53

"113, unit 113. Respond to the University Hospital ER in reference to an assault. Complainant is the ER staff. Homeless male was brought in suffering injuries to head and body. No suspect info. Respond code 2."

"113 copies," Shook said. "We just left the hospital. We'll turn around and go back to the ER. You can go ahead and mark us 10-23 (on scene)."

"10-4, 113. 10-23 at 1412hrs."

Park drove around the block and pulled up to the ER entrance. It was a tight fit in the tunnel where the ambulances and police cars parked. Park generally liked to park outside of the tunnel and walk in. That way he didn't have to back and forth the police SUV into a space for 5 minutes and he got some cardio from the walk. Plus, there was a food cart on the sidewalk for when he gave in to temptation.

Park stopped to see what the special was today, while Shook surreptitiously looked at the piece of paper that Garcia had given him. Park caught him and pretended to snatch it out of his hand. "Do it and someone will be taking an assault report from *you* inside." Park laughed and walked on into the ER, forgoing the food cart for now.

Park and Shook walked into the controlled chaos of the ER. Since this was a teaching hospital, as well as a nationally renowned Trauma Center, they were nearly constantly busy. Medical students learning their trade, from interns to residents to fellows. And those were just the medical school students. Nurses, physical therapists, respiratory therapists, x-ray techs, and the list went on and on. Medics and corpsman also trained here since there was no shortage of gunshot wounds to treat and practice on. At times it was overwhelming, even to Park who had years of experience in coming down here.

Park walked over to one of the nurse's stations across from the trauma bays and asked about the assault patient. The nurse was getting ready to answer when the portable phone she wore clipped to the back of her scrubs rang. She held up a finger at Park and listened to the caller, making notes on a pad in front of her. She hung up without saying goodbye and said to Park, "Sorry. Crazy as usual. You here for the homeless guy?"

"Yep," said Park. "Hold on a sec. Hey! Doctor Torrez? Doctor Torrez!! Can you come talk to the police for a second about the homeless guy?" Park looked over at the middle bay and a man he assumed was Dr. Torrez came over, looking a bit harried. "Yes, how can I help you gentlemen?"

"Just trying to find out what's going on with the assault over there." Park nodded to the curtained off section of the middle bay. "He's not doing so well," Torrez said. "Someone really pounded on him. It looks like he may have a skull fracture towards the back of his skull. We'll need to take him for a CAT scan to see if he's got a brain bleed. He's had a few teeth knocked out and I'd be surprised if he doesn't lose an eye."

"Goddamn," Shook said.

"Yes," said the doctor. "He may also have a broken radius and ulna of the right arm. We'll know more once he's x-rayed. Are you two handling this? With injuries this severe, a detective usually comes down."

"We'll see what's going on first, then give them a call," said Park. "You think his injuries are life-threatening?"

"Oh, yes. Most definitely because of the possible skull fracture."

"Ok. Shook? Go out and get Rooney on the radio or cell phone. Let him know what's going on and ask him to give Major Crimes a call." There was so much electrical equipment in the ER that many times it was impossible to transmit via radio or cell phone from within the ER. Shook nodded and walked outside.

"Mind if I go take a look at him before he goes to the CAT?" Park asked.

"No problem, I'll see him again when they get done with the scan. Unless he goes right to surgery, that is." Torrez turned and walked over into the first bay, shifting focus to another crisis. Park walked over to the curtain and stepped inside of it, then looked down at the victim. *Fuck.* It was Wassmer, the ex-police officer.

CHAPTER 54

"How'd Cindy find him so fast?" Peck asked. Danny had picked her up at the courthouse after he left the Mexican joint. He was hoping when he called her that she'd be tied up and he could tell Cindy to go ahead and grab Defreitis without them. He'd seen plenty of arrests and would have preferred to enjoy his burrito bowl, especially since he paid full price. But it wasn't meant to be; Peck was done with court and said that she'd be waiting on the courthouse steps for Danny, and to hurry the hell up. So, Danny gave the bowl to a guy with a cardboard sign that read, 'Homeless, not helpless. Anything helps.' The guy had a mangy looking dog on a leash beside him, so hopefully he'd share. He'd picked her up from the courthouse five minutes later and they were on their way to Shockoe.

"I'm not sure how she does it," Danny said. "I know she uses cell phone stuff, but since we took his last one, he must have gotten another, and she figured out what the new number was. Assuming he got a new number and didn't just switch it to a new phone."

"Well, however she does it, this should be the last time we need to pick him up. With the blood evidence, asshole

Reggie's testimony, and the gun, we're pretty solid," Peck said.

Danny's phone rang, and he hit the speakerphone button and tossed the phone in a cupholder so both he and Peck could hear. "Hey, Cindy. We're a few blocks away."

"Ok. He's rolling. We just took a left on Main St. If he stays on Main, we'll initiate the traffic stop right there near the county line. The road opens up some and there aren't any houses or apartments right there, in case he decides to run."

"Alright," Danny said. "What are you driving? The Dodge SUV?"

"Yep, that's us."

"We're a few blocks behind you. Once you get him stopped, we'll hang back until he's cuffed. Just tell us when and we'll come up and have a look at him and the car," Danny said.

"No problem. Ok, get ready; we're going to light him up."

As Danny and Peck watched, the hidden light bars in the Dodge lit up; front, back, and sides. Danny had a hard time seeing what Defreitis was driving since it was blocked by Cindy's SUV. He assumed it was another rental. Since he had Peck in the car with him, he dropped back a little further. Cindy had already lined up a marked unit to assist in the traffic stop and it was in front of her.

Danny saw a grey colored car pull over to the right almost immediately as the police lights came on. The patrol SUV stopped behind and to the left, while Cindy's SUV stayed to the right. Danny stopped in the middle of the road, about five car lengths back and turned on his rear deck lights; he wanted to make sure no civilian cars drove by while the arrest was being made.

The grey car sat, idling. Danny could see the back of a head in the driver's seat, but it wasn't moving. The police radio had gone silent and all he heard was the clicking of his rear lights, blocking traffic behind.

CHAPTER 55

Shook was still on the phone when Park came barreling out of the ER. "C'mon," he said to Shook. "Now." Shook hustled to catch up with him and ended his call.

"What the hell, Park? I was finishing up with Rooney. Where are we going? Don't we need to wait on the detectives?"

Park ignored him, got in the car, and started it up. Shook stood on the sidewalk and said, "Park? We need to wait here to brief the detectives. What's going on?"

"He's going in for a CAT scan and that takes a half hour. If it goes well. His won't because he's so fucked up, so he'll probably go right to surgery. Which means hours. I'm not waiting around when I know who did it. You coming or staying? Make a fucking decision."

Shook got in the car and Park took off.

* * *

"How do you know who did it?" Shook asked. "And do you know that guy? The victim?"

"Yeah, it's Wassmer."

"That 10-96 cop who taught you at the academy?" Shook queried.

"Yes. And don't call him 10-96 again. Got it?"

"Ok, ok. Sorry. No offense. Watch the bike!" A bicyclist had merged into the traffic lane and Park had almost nailed him. Park swerved around him, tooting the air horn, and getting the middle finger thrown at him for it. "Asshole," Park muttered under his breath.

"So.......how do you know who did it?" Shook asked again.

"When I went into the room and saw it was Wassmer, I leaned over him to tell him it was going to be ok and a cop was with him. Just like I did for Garcia. He was just kind of mumbling, but then I made out what he was saying, 'Get off on the right foot officer, get off on the right foot officer'."

"Yeah? So?" Shook said.

"I know who says that," Park said, as he hit the lights and siren.

CHAPTER 56

"What do you think he's doing in there?" Peck asked, as a car horn sounded behind them, the driver pissed off that the road was blocked.

"Beats me," said Danny. He'd rolled his window down and could hear the patrol officer on the SUV's PA system ordering Defreitis to come out of the car, hands up. The car horn honked again; this time the driver was really laying on it. "Impatient ass motherfucker," Danny said, looking over his shoulder. "Hold on, I'll be right back," he said as he opened the car door and stepped out to confront the honker. "Danny? He's getting out of the car," Peck said. Danny turned and looked as Defreitis got out of the car with a pistol in his hand and immediately start shooting, right to left.

* * *

It all happened in the blink of an eye; Defreitis missed the marked SUV completely, but his bullets found their mark with Danny's car. Danny was struck on the meaty part of his upper right arm, then another round hit him in the hip, his gun and holster taking the bullet. Defreitis swung the gun to the left, steadily pulling the trigger. Bullets shattered the windshield of Danny's car and then hit the driver's side mirror of Cindy's Dodge, but that was as far as they got. When Defreitis got out of his car, the Marshal who'd tailed him into the strip club the first time rolled out of the passenger side of the SUV. By the time Defreitis had shot up the windshield of Danny's car, the Marshal had gotten a good sight picture on Defreitis and fired twice; both rounds hitting Defreitis in his head, ending the gunfight as fast as it had begun.

* * *

"Peck!!" Danny yelled, ignoring the pain in his arm and hip. He ran to the open door and saw Peck staring straight ahead, bleeding from the chest, stomach, and arm. She looked over at Danny and her head slumped to her chest.

"Cindy!! Help!! Peck's been shot!!"

Cindy ran over, holstering her pistol and looking in the car. "Oh shit!! Danny, get in there beside her! I'll drive to the hospital!" A Marshal rushed over and looked at Peck, "Oh, shit. Here, take these," she said, handing Danny packets of field dressings. Danny ripped them open and started pressing them against Peck's chest and stomach. "Hang in there, Peck. We're taking you to the hospital. C'mon Peck. Hang in there!"

Danny jumped over into the back seat so that he could hold the dressings in place from behind her. Cindy got in the driver's side, threw the car in gear, and took off west down Main Street, siren howling.

"796 to radio!! We've had shots fired, suspect is down! We've got a civilian injured. We're transporting her to the ER. ETA of three minutes. Call ahead and let them know we're coming in hot!!"

"Radio copies. Calling ahead now."

"Hang in there, Peck. Jesus, hang in there," Danny said, blood soaking through the dressing onto his hands.

CHAPTER 57

Get off on the right foot officer. The last time Park had heard that phrase had been a few months ago, while standing in line at a store. The odd guy with tattoos on his neck. Once Park had left the store, the guy had talked to him for 10 minutes, mainly just spouting out nonsense.

"You sure it's the guy you're thinking about? It's a pretty common phrase, you know," Shook asked.

"Yeah, but the way he said it? With the emphasis on the word *officer*? There's just something about it that feels right."

All of the sudden, they heard on the radio:

"796 to radio!! We've had shots fired, suspect is down! We've got a civilian injured. We're transporting her to the ER. ETA of three minutes. Call ahead and let them know we're coming in hot!!"

"Radio copies. Calling ahead now."

"Damn," Shook said. "Full moon or something this afternoon. What the hell?" Then he grabbed ahold of the 'oh shit' bar on the roof of the SUV as Park made a tight, right turn onto Brook Road, horns honking at them from behind.

Park got the car back under control and said, "That's the store up on the right. Where the employee was killed about 10 years ago."

"I was like a freshman in high school 10 years ago, grandpa," Shook said.

"There he is," Park said, slowing down and taking a right into the parking lot of a laundromat next to the store. There was a vacant business building next to the laundry and it looked like someone had turned it into an outside gym. There were rusty weight benches scattered around and barbells with cracked, grey, plastic coated concrete weight plates. There were a few hexagonal dumbbells, dinged up and battered, lined up on a wooden rack built to hold something else.

The guy Park was talking about was doing dips on one of those 'tower of power' racks: a device for doing pull-ups, dips, and pushups. He was lowering himself smoothly, then pushing himself back up, triceps well-defined and pecs popping.

"Fuck," Shook said, "When'd The Rock move to Richmond and become homeless?"

Park ignored him and pulled up right inside the perimeter of the outside gym, knocking over one of the benches with the bumper of the SUV. He got out of the SUV and walked right over to the guy, all attention focused on one thing: the red, Marine Corps hat the guy was wearing.

CHAPTER 58

For the whole ride through the far east end of Richmond, then into downtown where the university ER was, Danny held onto Peck, trying to staunch the flow of blood. He'd been having little success. "Goddammit, Cindy, drive faster!!"

"Us getting in a wreck isn't going to help her, Danny, so shut the fuck up!!" She drove straight down Main Street, picking up two RPD motor officers at Fifteenth Street, who escorted her the last ten or so blocks to the ER. She pulled into the ER tunnel, opening her door before the car came to a stop.

ER staff was ready and waiting with a gurney and yanked on the passenger door to get Peck out, but it was locked. "Unlock the fucking door," a nurse said calmly, but with authority. Cindy ran back around to her open door and hit the *unlock* button on the armrest. The staff reached in and got Peck under her shoulders, then moved her onto the gurney.

One of the doctors got up on the side of the gurney and started doing chest compressions while another doc put an Ambu bag over Peck's face and started squeezing it. The rest of the staff started pushing the gurney into the ER, the doc doing compressions riding on the side of the gurney. "Go with her, Danny," Cindy said. Danny ran alongside the gurney and went with them into the ER. The doors closed, and a red light mounted to the ceiling just outside of the ER suite turned on.

Cindy stood there for a minute and brought her breathing under control. The motor guys had dismounted their bikes and were standing there, white helmets still on, looking at the car; shot up windshield and hood, a thin stream of smoke coming from the grill, blood soaked front passenger seat with used field dressings scattered on the floor and seats. "Jesus Christ," one of them said, "It looks like one of the medevac Humvees from Iraq."

Cindy put her hand to her forehead and leaned against the wall, the adrenalin starting to dissipate from her system. "Either of you guys got a cigarette?"

CHAPTER 59

"What's your fucking problem, officer?" the guy said as Park approached him. Shook was a few steps behind Park and moved over to the right of Park, staying silent.

"What's your name, *sir?*" Park said, matching the inflection and emphasis of the guy's voice. Shook looked around and saw that they'd drawn the attention of a few other homeless guys, some making their way over to hear the conversation between Park and the suspect.

"113 on channel 4 to radio?" Shook transmitted.

"Go ahead, 113."

"We'll be out with a few parties beside the laundromat at Brook and Azalea. Start one more unit this way, non-emergency."

"10-4, 113. Unit to back 113?"

"K7's got him from Westbrook and Brook," K9 officer Ashley Burton said. She and her partner, a German Shepherd named Dallas, had been in the area for a PR.

"10-4, K7. 1534hrs."

"You don't need to know my name. What's this about? I'm not bothering anyone," returned the big guy.

"I didn't say you were bothering anyone. I just asked your name. What's the problem? You got warrants?" Park asked.

"I don't have any 29s," the guy responded. Once the neighborhood guys were stopped enough times, they picked up on the meanings of the '10 codes' and could translate. It was a two-way street because cops picked up on street slang the same way.

"Only way for me to find out is by running you. Now what's your name?" Park asked again.

"K7 is 10-23," Burton said as she pulled into the lot. She left her car running and cracked the window of the rear compartment so Dallas could stick his nose out. She got out and walked over to Shook, raising her chin in greeting. He did the same in return.

"Oh, now you're going to turn the dog loose on me?" the guy remarked. Burton ignored him, and Park repeated, "Name. Now."

"Whatever. It's Douglas Fairfield. No middle name."

"Soc?" Park queried, pronounced 'sosh' with a hard o; short for social security number. Fairfield gave it to him, and Burton said that she'd run it. She went back to her SUV and sat down with the door open, leaving one leg out on the running board. A few more homeless guys had approached, drawn to Fairfield raising his voice and the second patrol SUV arriving on scene.

"You guys need to step back a few," Shook directed the gathering men. Burton had noticed the group gathering and got on the radio.

"Ah, K7 to radio? A couple more units over here. Still non-emergency. We've got a bit of a crowd gathering and we don't want to get surrounded out here."

"10-4, K7. Need a couple more units to the laundromat lot near Brook and Azalea. Non-emergency for right now."

"412 responding," answered one officer.

"413 from Westbrook and Hermitage," said another.

"10-4, 412 and 413," said the dispatcher. "Supervisor copy?"

"405, copies. That's a 1st precinct unit at Brook and Azalea?" the sergeant asked. The intersection of Brook and Azalea was miles from the 1st precinct boundary.

"10-4," the dispatcher confirmed.

"Ok, radio," the sergeant said, "I'm 10-17 to their location." The sergeant had been at DEC picking up some paperwork. He had been planning to head back to the precinct to start wrapping things up and head home, but now he had to see what that this 1st precinct officer was doing in *his* precinct. Just once he'd like to get off on time.....

Burton was looking at her MDT for any information that may be coming up on Fairfield. Dallas gave a low growl from the back seat. Unlike Thunder, Dallas was a more mellow fellow. Whereas Thunder barked whenever and wherever he could, Dallas preferred to save his voice and do a slow build up. Now he was letting Burton know that things may start getting hairy, so she needed to pay attention. She looked over at Park and Shook, then back at the screen. The MDTs were running a bit slow today. She looked back over and saw that four guys were inching closer to Park and Shook; not sneaking up on them behind their backs, just moving in closer. She rolled Dallas' window down to the halfway point and told him to speak.

"WOOOFWOOFWOOFWOOOFWOOOOF!!!"

The guys backed away from Shook. She went back to the MDT screen.

Park heard the K9 barking and was confident that Shook and the K9 team had his back. "I see you got some injuries to your knuckles, there," Park pointed out, nodding at Fairfield's hands. "What happened?"

"Training, motherfucker," Fairfield replied. "Knuckle pushups. MMA conditioning. Looks like you could use some conditioning, *officer*."

Park inched closer to him, keeping his gun side turned slightly away from the bigger man. Fairfield inched back a step as Park said, "Is that what you did to Wassmer? Some *conditioning?*"

Fairfield licked his lips and moved his head from side to side, as if loosening up. The four guys who'd backed up when Dallas barked, now started moving in again when they saw Park get in Fairfield's face.

"I said, *back the fuck up*," Shook repeated. He pulled his OC canister off of his duty belt and started to shake it. He moved his neck from side to side, too.

* * *

Burton saw a warrant showing out of Richmond for Fairfield; a misdemeanor failure to appear charge out of criminal court. It wasn't a big deal, but it was an arrestible offense. Dallas was growling again, keeping a close eye on the group approaching Shook. "Easy, boy," she said, closing the door and walking back over to Shook.

"412 and 413 are 10-23," one of the officers said as both black and white Ford Tauruses rolled into the parking lot.

The 4th precinct officers, Larry Newton (412) and Alan Joyner (413) got out of their cars and began to walk over. Newton noticed the crowd forming and leaned back into his car for the large fogger canister of OC. Then he joined Joyner, Shook, and Burton.

Newton looked at Shook's little OC canister and held his much larger one up next to it. Burton noticed and rolled her eyes, then walked over to Park.

The additional officers had drawn additional people to the gathering crowd, which happens often. Newton had the OC fogger in his left hand, aiming it at the crowd's feet. If any of them started to make a move to bum rush the officers, he'd let loose the fogger at their feet.

"Stop hassling D!" one guy in the crowd yelled, apparently Fairfield's nickname. "Fucking cops, always picking on people for no reason. Motherfuckers!" shouted another. A low murmur started rising from the crowd, people starting to get into the name-calling. The cops were becoming outnumbered, three to one. Newton got the fogger ready; Shook reconsidered his smaller canister and took out his ASP, but didn't deploy it yet. Joyner did the same.

"Park?" Burton said.

"Yeah?"

"He's got a failure to appear out of the city. Confirmed through the Warrants desk. They have the paper in hand."

Park smiled and said, "You're under arrest; turn around and……," which was as far as he got before Fairfield punched him right in the face. Park staggered backwards a step, then he and Burton pounced on Fairfield as the crowd lunged forward, while Newton deployed the fogger. Shook and Joyner extended their ASPs, and the fight was on.

CHAPTER 60

"You can't come in here like that," the voice said through the call box.

"Like what?" Danny said.

"With all that blood on your shirt. Are you ok?" the voice asked.

Danny looked down and saw that his shirt was stained in multiple places with Peck's blood. He'd washed his hands before he'd left the hospital, but he'd forgotten about his shirt. His car was technically part of the crime scene, so when he left the ER he'd walked down the hill to the Justice Center. He was surprised no one had called 911 on him; a hollow-eyed guy walking down the street with blood all over his shirt. Maybe they'd seen the badge and gun on his belt and just went on their way, shaking their heads about RVA.

He looked around and saw a garbage can by the main entrance of the Justice Center, so he walked over to it. He unbuttoned his shirt and threw it away in the trash can. He checked out his reflection in the glass of the entrance and thought he looked ok, like one of the plainclothes Narcotics detectives who worked in jeans and t-shirts. Or the FBI agents who favored tactical pants and button down short sleeved shirts that were meant to conceal their weapons, but never did. He didn't notice the deputy at the front desk watching him look at himself in the reflection. The deputy had picked up the phone and was getting ready to call 911, when he noticed the badge and gun. He put the phone back down, but kept an eye on Danny until he had walked back to the side entrance.

Danny pushed the intercom button again and waited until the voice said, "Who're you here to see?"

"Reggie Taylor."

There was a pause, then the voice came back on and said, "Make sure you get a gun box when you come in the lobby. If you have any ammunition or other weapons, put them in there, too. Have your ID ready."

Danny nodded absently and the door buzzed, letting him inside.

* * *

Danny was at the table, staring at his hands when a deputy tapped on the glass. Danny looked up and nodded, and the deputy opened the door and Reggie walked in.

"Sit down, fucker," Danny said, without affect in his voice.

Reggie gave him an odd look, but sat down in front of him. Danny didn't say anything else, just sat there staring at Reggie. Reggie tried to hold the stare, but eventually gave up.

"What do you want, man? Why are you just sitting there? You came to see me," Reggie asked. Danny still said nothing.

"Fuck this," Reggie said and got up to walk out.

"I said, sit.....the.....fuck.....DOWN!!!!" Danny screamed the last word, veins standing out on his neck and forehead.

"Ok, man, ok. I'm sitting down. What the fuck's your problem?" Reggie asked, sitting down and crossing his arms over his chest.

"What's *my* problem?" asked Danny. "Is that what you asked? What's *my* problem?"

"Uh, yeah," answered Reggie. "That info I gave you was good, right? I said I'd testify. You and that bitch prosecutor got what you wanted. Why're you coming in here acting all crazy and shit?" For the first time, Reggie seemed to notice that Danny was in a t-shirt. "Why're you dressed like that anyway? You look all fucked up and out of it." Reggie leaned in and whispered, "You high or something?"

Danny sprung forward and grabbed Reggie by his collar and slammed him down on the ground, landing on top of him. He'd knocked the table over as he grabbed him, so that now they were both tangled up in its legs. Danny was vaguely aware of an alarm going off somewhere in the jail, but he was too concentrated on holding Reggie against the floor to notice.

"I wanted to let you know in person, you fucking scumbag," Danny said. "Your deal is off. We don't need your fucking testimony because Defreitis is dead. You're gonna rot in here, Reggie, until you serve all your time." Danny heard feet pounding down the hallway outside of the room. He realized that the alarm was probably for him, either to help him or to help Reggie.

"Get him offa me!! Help, this guy's gone crazy!!" Reggie was screaming as the deputies appeared at the door.

Danny let go of him just as the deputies came into the room and pulled Danny away from Reggie. "One more thing, Reggie?" Danny said over the shoulders of the deputies who were tugging him out of the room. "Don't you ever call her a bitch again."

CHAPTER 61

Park leaned against the rear bumper of the ambulance with an ice pack on his jaw. He moved his tongue around in his mouth, checking his gums for any missing or loose teeth. All present and accounted for. He had the shoulder mic of his walkie clipped onto his magazine pouch since his shirt lapel had not survived the fight. He had a hole in the knee of his right pants leg, and a raspberry on the same knee from kneeling on the ground, trying to get Fairfield cuffed.

The air smelled faintly like oranges, the left-over aroma from the OC fog. Another ambulance was parked about ten feet away, an assembly line of prisoners getting OC washed out of their eyes and off their faces by medics. After they got rinsed off, they were moved over to the back of the patrol wagon, referred to as the paddy wagon by many generations of cops, where they'd be taken to the Justice Center and charged with disorderly conduct, maybe assault on a police officer if they kept being assholes.

Fairfield may have gotten the first punch in, but Park had been hit before and gave much better than he got; he'd had Fairfield on the ground quickly after that initial punch. The other homeless guys just half-assed it once Fairfield was under control and the OC fog sealed the deal.

Shook walked over to Park and said, "How're you feeling? He got you a pretty good one. I think I may have gotten it on the BWC. I may blackmail you with it."

Burton walked over as Shook continued, "Or maybe I'll sell it online. Remember that horrible show 'Bumfight' or whatever it was? I bet if you throw a big Korean cop who looks like Bolo from all those 70's and 80's movies in the mix, I could sell a million copies."

Park shifted the ice pack from his jaw to the back of his neck and said, "First of all, no one says 'bum' anymore. At least you're not supposed to. And Bolo Yeung is Chinese, not Korean. You're getting your Asians all mixed up."

"Whatever," Burton said. "Hey, how's Sharon? She and Thunder usually work with your platoon over in Church Hill, don't they?"

"Yeah," Park said. "She's doing ok. They're making her talk to a shrink about the shooting over at the mall parking lot, but that's just normal OIS stuff. I expect they'll clear her pretty quickly from it. That guy did shoot up a couple of Trooper cars *and* hit Thunder, too."

"Thunder was lucky," Burton said, ruffling the fur at Dallas' neck. "I don't know what I'd do if my girl here got shot."

Park nodded and looked over and saw a patrolman standing next to a sergeant, pointing over at Park. The sergeant nodded, then started walking over to him. He didn't look happy. "Oh boy," said Burton. "Here comes Sgt. Brown. He was getting ready to EOT when the melee happened. He looks pissed. I'm out. If you see Sharon, let her know I asked about her. I'll shoot her a text later. Good luck." Then she and Dallas walked off toward their SUV.

Shook said, "Well, I'll let you talk to the sergeant in private. I'm going to call and check on Garcia. I'll be in the car," leaving Park alone to explain to the 4th Precinct sergeant why the sergeant wasn't going to make it to dinner on time.

CHAPTER 62

Danny was sitting down in the Investigations section of the Justice Center, watching as one of the investigators was typing up the incident report. Danny wasn't in custody per se, but wasn't exactly allowed to leave yet either. Technically he could have been charged with assaulting Reggie, but the investigator, Danny couldn't remember his name, said that he'd talk to Reggie later and see if he wanted to prosecute; he doubted that he would. Danny appreciated the effort but didn't care if he was charged or not; it felt good trying to tie a knot in Reggie's narrow ass.

Just outside the office, Danny saw Ryan Dean, his sergeant, talking to one of the Justice Center's majors. Most of the high-ranking officers in the Sheriff's Office (the agency that was responsible for the jails and prisoners in Richmond) were former RPD. The major was slamming his fist into his hand over and over, and Ryan was holding both hands out in front of him, palms up, like trying to push the major back. Danny couldn't hear what was being said because the glass was sound proof, but it was still interesting to watch. Ryan pointed to his own shirt, then in the room to Danny's. The major turned to look at Danny, then back to Ryan. Ryan then pointed to his arm, then back at Danny again, probably indicating where Danny had been grazed by one of Defreitis' bullets. Finally, the major tapped on the glass, getting his investigator's attention. "I'll be right back," the guy said to Danny, then popped his head outside the door. He nodded a couple of times, then came back in. "You're good to go, Danny. Your sergeant's going to give you a ride. Take it easy. Sorry about Peck." He offered Danny his hand and Danny shook it, then walked out to Ryan. "C'mon Danny, let's go," Ryan said, "I'll take you back to the hospital." Danny simply nodded and followed Ryan out of the building.

CHAPTER 63

Sgt. Brown walked away from Park, shaking his head. Most of the units were clearing up and heading back into service. Park looked around, trying to find a trashcan so he could throw away the ice pack, which had proceeded to become a warm water sack. Not having any luck, he opened the door and tossed it on the back floor of the car. "How's Garcia doing?" he asked.

"Lots better," Shook answered. "She wanted me to give you the finger because of the 'lopsided face' remark you made at the hospital. I told her I would, but you've had a rough day, so I won't."

"Thanks," Park replied, looking over his left shoulder in preparation for pulling out into traffic. Which presented the perfect opportunity to make good on Garcia's request; Shook gave the side of Park's face the finger, then dropped his hand back to his side.

"I saw that," Park said as the radio squawked:

"Radio to 113?"

"Go ahead, radio," Shook answered.

"Can you 10-25 unit 792 at HQ, 3rd floor?"

"10-12 a second, radio," Shook said.

"You want me to drop you off at HQ while I go help with all those homeless guys at lock-up?" Shook asked.

"Yeah, that'll work. I think they took Fairfield to HQ to interview him about Wassmer. I'll see what's up there and you head on down to lock-up so the 4th Precinct guys don't get tied up with something we started," Park replied.

"113 to radio? I'm dropping my partner off at HQ, then heading down to lock-up to relieve the 4th Precinct officers."

"10-4, 113."

"Was Sgt. Brown pissed?" Shook asked, as Park started driving to HQ.

"A little at first," Park replied. "But when I told him about Wassmer, he was cool. He remembered Wassmer from the academy."

"You heard how Wassmer's doing?" Shook asked.

"Not yet," Park said. "After I meet with the detective, I'm going to catch a ride over there and check on him. I'll call your cell when I'm done. If you're still tied up at lock-up, I'll catch a ride back to the precinct."

Park pulled up in front of HQ and got out of the car. "Put my warbag in the trunk if I don't see you before EOT," he said, as Shook came around to the driver's side. "You got it," Shook replied. "Let me know what happened with that shooting where the civilian got hit. I heard they got the bad guy, so that's good. Later." Park walked into HQ.

CHAPTER 64

Ryan and Danny walked into the hospital, and right away, Danny knew Peck was gone. When he'd stumbled away down to the Justice Center, the lobby and halls were packed with people, waiting for an update. Now the lobby was practically empty, just a few people sitting in the waiting room chairs, looking shell-shocked with tears in their eyes.

One of Peck's co-workers, another prosecutor, came up to Danny and said, "She's gone, Danny. They couldn't save her. Why did you have her with you in the car, Danny? Why?"

Danny took two steps back and collapsed in a seat, head in his hands.

Ryan led Peck's co-worker away, speaking softly to her, convincing her to give Danny some space. "You son of a *bitch*!! You got her KILLED!!" the woman sobbed, then ran off down the hall.

Danny didn't move or react; he just sat there, head in his hands, rocking back and forth. Ryan looked at him, then stepped into a side hallway and dialed a number. "Park? It's Ryan. Danny needs you."

CHAPTER 65

Det. Dave Watts was waiting for Park in the reception area on the third floor of HQ. Park had seen him around a few times and had heard Danny talk about him; he seemed like an ok guy. "Hey Park. I just got done interviewing Fairfield. He gave it up," Watts said.

"Oh yeah?' Park said. "Good job. So, what's that guy's problem? Why'd he go after Wassmer?"

"Well, I think he's a little on the mental side. And you know, Wassmer is too," Watts said. "Regardless, Wassmer didn't deserve to get a beat down like he did. Oh, and he's going to make it. Though he's going to lose an eye."

"He may make some more money begging, wearing the Marine Corps hat *and* an eye patch," Park reasoned.

"Seriously," agreed Watts. "But anyway, Fairfield said that he's never liked cops and had just recently found out that Wassmer was a cop. Apparently Wassmer's been beaten up before for the same reason?" Watts guessed.

"Yeah," Park confirmed. "He keeps it on the down low when he's in his right mind, but I've heard he sometimes brings up his old cop days when his meds are out of whack. That's what happened to him last time."

"Wonder why he doesn't just leave Richmond?" Watts wondered.

"This is his home," Park replied. "You know RVA has a pull that you can't ignore."

"If I got my ass beat so bad I could see the light, *twice*, I'd be like 'fuck RVA, I'm gone.'" Watts said. "And I was born and raised here."

Before Park could respond, his phone rang. "Park," he answered. He listened for a second, then said, "Where? Ok." Park hung up. "I gotta go," and left to go to the hospital.

EPILOGUE

Thunder was busy tearing up a fresh piece of car tire when the doorbell rang. Most dogs would go nuts, barking and running around like their ass was on fire and their tail was catching. But then that gave away the element of surprise, didn't it? If someone was coming into his house uninvited and up to no good, he wanted to make sure he got a nice, big, juicy bite out of them before they ran away screaming.

"Easy, bud. It's just dad," Sharon said as she went to open the door. Thunder would just wait and see about that.....

Sharon opened the door and Park walked in, offering his cheek for a kiss. Sharon obliged and shut the door. "You've got a key, dad. Why do you keep ringing the doorbell?"

"Because you're an adult, number one, and I don't want to walk in on anything you may have going on..." He fake-shuddered. "And, because I don't want to have to break your dog's neck if he tried to bite me if I came in unannounced." Thunder growled, then turned his back on Park, getting back to his car tire.

Sharon rolled her eyes, then took a seat on the couch, folding her legs under her. Park got a little nostalgic seeing her sitting like that; he remembered her sitting like that when she was a little girl. He sat on the floor and said, "C'mere dog." Thunder ignored him and kept chewing.

"How's Danny? I heard about Peck," Sharon asked.

"He's pretty fucked up," Park replied. "He and Peck weren't really friends, but they worked well on cases together. His sergeant told me that one of her coworkers freaked out a little on Danny, blaming him for Peck being there when they went to get Defreitis. But the sergeant also told me that's how Peck was; always wanting to be in the middle of stuff."

"I met her a couple of times on cases," Sharon said. "She was pretty aggressive. Really seemed to love her job."

"Yeah. He's got no issues with her being with him when they went to arrest the fucker. As far as the department is concerned, anyway. He's going to have to deal with his personal guilt, though. Along with her death," Park said.

"Where's he now?" Sharon asked.

"I gave him a ride home in his new unmarked and Shook picked me up from Danny's house. He's going to take a week or so off to deal with all of it. I'll swing by in the morning and we'll get a list going for his deck. I'm going to try and convince him to put a roof on it," Park said.

"C'mere, you fucking grumpy ass dog!" Park said again. Thunder thumped his tail once, then went back to chewing. "What an asshole," Park muttered, getting two tail thumps in return.

"How're you doing, kiddo? Danny's not the only one under some stress," Park asked.

"You know, I'm actually doing pretty good. I was always fine with the shooting, but the baby case was still fucking up my head some," she answered.

"Language, please," Park scolded.

Sharon sighed and continued, "*Messing* up my head. Anyway, talking to the department shrink had helped with that. I think IA's going to clear me in another month or so over the shooting. Especially since they're almost positive it's the second bank robber. A Major Crimes guy goes to my gym and told me that the guy I shot? Nobody liked his ass. This detective talked to the NYPD cops, who talked to people in his old neighborhood. The dude Abad shot back when the robbery happened was this guy's only friend. Everyone else up there couldn't stand him. And get this."

Park was listening to her, but creeping his hand toward Thunder's tail.

"The NYPD guys are pretty sure he killed a guy up there, before coming back down here. They found one of those app drivers dead behind a dumpster; knife sticking out of the back of his head like the stem of an apple."

"Nice image," said Park.

"It shouldn't be much longer before they know for sure," she continued. "They're gonna send my dead guy's DNA card over to the lab for a one-to-one comparison with evidence they recovered from the bank."

"Uh-huh," Park said, hand just inches from Thunder's tail.

"Once the results are back, I should get cleared by the prosecutor's office, then the department. After that, Thunder and I are back in business."

"Gotcha!" Park triumphed, grabbing Thunder's tail in a tight grip and giving it a gentle tug. Thunder let out a loud bark, whipped his tail from Park's grip, and pounced on his chest, Park holding Thunder's head and wiggling it back and forth.

Sharon started looking through her phone while her boys were wrestling around on the floor. They eventually stopped, Thunder going back to chewing on his tire while Park went to the bathroom. After a flush and the sound of hand washing, Park came out of the bathroom and told her that he had to get on home.

"Hey," Sharon said as he was heading out the door. "Did Shook ever ask out that Trooper?"

"As a matter of fact……," Park said.

* * *

Shook pulled up in front of the apartment complex and checked the address on the text one more time; yep, he was at the right place. He saw a VSP cruiser parked under one of the covered parking spots, so he guessed this was it.

Looking at his reflection in the rear-view mirror, he made a few minor adjustments, then got out and locked his car. He saw a couple of guys walking toward him in the parking lot, and he automatically bladed his gun side away from them. As they came abreast of him, they both smiled and waved, then headed on to wherever it was they were going.

"Can't turn it off, can you?" a voice to his left said, slightly startling him. Garcia stepped out into the parking lot streetlight, dressed in jeans and a tan, sleeveless top. Her hair was up in a ponytail and she wore a pair of plain, simple sandals. She took his breath away.

"Nope. I can't," he said.

"Neither can I," she responded. "Let's go, Shook. I'm starving. Take me to dinner."

END OF TOUR

Check out the first chapter of *The Last to Suffer*, the next book in the Danny and Park adventure series. Available at Amazon and on the author's website:

Dannyandparknovels.com

THE LAST TO SUFFER

A Danny and Park novel
James P. Baynes

Prelude

December 24th, 1995

"116, I'm 10-23 on Bethel St," Officer Danny Jacobs advised radio.

"10-4, 116, 2345hrs. Use caution, male half is possibly armed with a knife."

"115 to 116? I'm about a minute out. Wait for me before you go in," Master Patrolman Overstreet transmitted.

Danny wasn't waiting. The call was for an assault in progress, man versus woman. Danny walked up to the door and couldn't hear anything from the front room. He thought he heard some muffled noises from the back, though.

"116 to radio? Something's going on out back. I'm going back there. Gimme the air for a minute."

"Radio to 115, you copy? 116 will be in the rear."

"115 copies," Overstreet said, sounding pissed.

Keeping his hand on his gun, Danny took out his Maglite (it used 4 D-cell batteries and was a foot long. In addition to being extremely bright, it also made for a good door knocker and an additional weapon if necessary. Most cops rarely, if ever, carried their hickory nightstick) and held it in his left hand, with its base resting on his left shoulder. He got to the corner of the building and peeked around the edge.

There was a woman on her hands and knees, shaking her head and spitting out blood. Danny took his flashlight off his shoulder and slid it back into the steel ring on his belt. He grabbed his radio off of his belt and keyed the mic just as an arm wrapped around his neck from behind, cutting off his transmission. Danny immediately grabbed the arm with his left hand, right hand going to his holster to make sure the guy couldn't get his gun; the holster only had a snap to secure the gun in place.

The guy yanked Danny back and drove him into the bricks of the house. He yanked him back again and fell on the ground on top of Danny. Danny swiveled his hips around and was able to brace a foot against the brick wall and drove backwards, but the guy was strong and held Danny in place. Danny let go with his left hand and started throwing wild punches over his shoulder, hoping to connect with something soft on the guy; maybe his nose or throat. No dice.

Danny's vision started blurring and everything was getting red around the edges. The last things he heard were keys jingling and leather creaking. Then everything compressed down to a single pin-prick of light before dissolving into nothing.

* * *

When Danny came to, he was on the ground, right where he'd seen the woman when he came around the corner. One of the EMTs had his hand on his back and asked him if he was alright, a capsule of smelling salts held in his hand. Danny told him he was, then he saw Officer Overstreet and Sgt. Carlson standing off to the side, talking to the woman. The guy who'd jumped Danny was laying off to the side, hands cuffed behind his back and blood coming from his ears.

Overstreet and Carlson saw that he was back among the living and walked over to him. "I told you to wait, rookie," Overstreet said. "See what *happens when you don't listen to your senior officers. All rookies are just the same; come out of the academy fresh and shiny, don't know shit, but think you're super cop." Overstreet let loose a long stream of brown tobacco juice in the flowerbed beside the porch.*

Danny tried to say something, but it came out in a hoarse whisper. He tried again, "What about him?" nodding to the guy cuffed on the ground.

"What about him? Fuck him," Overstreet remarked. "He's going to the hospital, then to lock up. I had to hit him with my radio when I saw he had you all locked up. Took three thumps before he let go. That 3rd hit did a number on him, I reckon."

"Go inside and get yourself cleaned up, rookie. Grab some fucking water out of the sink and try to rinse that dirt off your fucking uniform. Don't drink any of it, though. It's probably full of iron or lead," Carlson said.

"And don't take too long either," Overstreet said. "I'm not hanging around the hospital for hours while this guy gets treated. That's all you. And you're welcome for saving your life."

"Thanks," Danny muttered, walking inside the apartment. He went into the hall bathroom and saw that there was dirt all over the front of his uniform shirt. He cupped his hands under the faucet and got as much off of his shirt as he could. There weren't any towels in the bathroom, so he walked into the living room, wiping his hands on the front of his pants.

On the dirty, yellow tiled floor slept two children; neither could have been over 5yrs old. No bed, no mattress, no pillows. Just a threadbare sheet. There was one strand of red and green Christmas lights, blinking on and off. No tree and no presents. It looked like they'd slept right through their mom getting beat up in the backyard. Maybe the mom had gone to the back of the apartment to keep the kids from hearing her getting beat up. Maybe this was her Christmas gift to them. "Hurry the fuck up, rookie! It's cold out here!" Overstreet bellowed from outside.

Danny walked out the back door and into the night to follow the ambulance down to the hospital. For the rest of his career Danny would remember those children sleeping on a bare floor in one of Richmond's most dangerous housing projects on Christmas Eve.

CHAPTER 1

Present day

"When's the last time you heard from her?" Unit 116, Officer Shook, asked the complainant. It was his first call of the day and a possible DOA. He really didn't want to get stuck with a decomposing body so soon after leaving Garcia's apartment. He still had the scent of her lotion in his nose and wasn't eager to have it replaced by decomp.

"It's been a few days. Maybe three?" the complainant, Kathy Lloyd, said. She lived a few hours away, near Virginia Beach, and had been trying to get in touch with her aunt but hadn't had any luck. She'd driven up from the beach and knocked on the door, but no one had answered. All the shades in the house were closed and she didn't have a key.

"How old is your aunt?" Unit 113, Master Officer Park asked her. Shook was the log unit and Park was his back-up. When Park had gotten there, he walked around checking the doors and trying to detect the smell of a dead body, but hadn't so far. That might be good news, or it might mean that Aunt Lloyd had recently died and was still fresh.

"She's 65," said Kathy. "And she's pretty healthy," she added.

Everyone's healthy until they aren't, Park thought. He was getting ready to shoot Danny a text and let him know he may have a dead one for him, then remembered that Danny had been transferred from the Homicide Unit.

"Do you give us permission to force our way into the house?" Shook asked.

"I think all we need to do is just yank open the storm door," Park added. "Since it's locked, she may have left the inside door unlocked. Shouldn't be too much damage."

"Sure, that's fine," Kathy replied. Park walked over to his SUV and got out a 'Permission to Search' form, filled it out, and asked Kathy to sign it. Then he wrote in the part about possibly damaging the door, which she initialed.

"Ok, wait over here by my car," Park said, then nodded at Shook.

"116 to radio?"

"Go ahead, 116."

"Hold the air for a minute. 113 and I are going to search the house."

"10-4, 116. All units stand by, air held."

Shook went up to the porch, grabbed a hold of the storm door handle, and gave it a solid yank. Nothing. He tried again, same result. Park came up behind him and gave it a tug and it popped right open.

"I loosened it for you," Shook said.

"I know," Park responded, pulling his gun and holding it down by his thigh. "Let's go."

Made in the USA
Columbia, SC
06 December 2023